About the author

Jennifer Stinton, writing under the pseudonym Genevieve, is a professional musician, a flautist, who has spent her life working in London orchestras and as a soloist, touring internationally.

Since childhood, she has always had a passion for writing both prose and poetry. Genevieve won a poetry competition aged sixteen and has continued to write throughout the following years. She has travelled extensively throughout her career as a musician and is able to draw on the many experiences that have affected her during these events and episodes.

A visit to Tereglio, a mountain village in the Apennine region of Tuscany, staying with some musician friends who reside there, inspired the opening of *Toscane*. The many adventures she experienced in this beautiful region coloured the language and narrative of her debut novel, which she hopes will be the first of many.

TOSCANE

Genevieve Stinton

TOSCANE

Vanguard Press

VANGUARD PAPERBACK

© Copyright 2021
Genevieve Stinton

The right of Genevieve Stinton to be identified as author of this work has been asserted by her in accordance with the Copyright, Designs and Patents Act 1988.

All Rights Reserved

No reproduction, copy or transmission of this publication may be made without written permission.
No paragraph of this publication may be reproduced, copied or transmitted save with the written permission of the publisher, or in accordance with the provisions of the Copyright Act 1956 (as amended).

Any person who commits any unauthorised act in relation to this publication may be liable to criminal prosecution and civil claims for damages.

A CIP catalogue record for this title is available from the British Library.

ISBN 978-1-80016-012-5

Vanguard Press is an imprint of
Pegasus Elliot MacKenzie Publishers Ltd.
www.pegasuspublishers.com

First Published in 2021

Vanguard Press
Sheraton House Castle Park
Cambridge England

Printed & Bound in Great Britain

Dedication

I would like to dedicate this book to my mother, Mary, who has always inspired my writing and in memory of my father, Ken, who taught me to never give up on my dreams.

Also to my daughters, Miranda and Bella, who have encouraged my endeavours as a writer.

Acknowledgements

Thank you to all the friends who supported me in getting this first novel published.

But he who dares not grasp the thorn
Should never crave the rose.

The Narrow Way, Anne Bronte

Chapter One

It was at that moment, in the heady atmosphere of the Tuscan mountains, that I needed to tell her story.

The rising sun had just begun to touch, with golden fingers, the densely wooded hills. Dark green foliage of pines and the paler shade of firs crowded the hills. Their beauty was present wherever you looked, but sometimes the over-powering presence of the forest could be suffocating. Relief was provided by the bare purple-headed peaks in the hazy distance. Stone villages perched precariously on the lower slopes and the terracotta roofs smouldered with a soft amber glow. While observing this tableau, the light gradually filtered down to disperse the shadows of the fragrant night, reaching the base of the hills glowing in the warm morning air.

Her reverie was broken suddenly by the tolling of the clanging village bell, a half-hourly reminder of the relentless passage of time. Perhaps she had thought time would stand still during her sojourn, in this enchanted place. The precious silence was interrupted by silver bird song, muted by the weight of the heavy summer air. The rasping sound of cicadas providing a soundtrack to the unfolding scene.

Where to begin? The potent question. Her life had never followed a planned route; like a small boat tossed on a stormy sea, she found a sheltered harbour from time to time, occasionally stemming the wanderlust of those eventful years.

At last, Marina had time to reflect on the past and possibly, for once, make decisions about the future. This was a new sensation for this impulsive creature. Her whole being exuded creative energy, from the unruly locks of her sun-streaked hair, to the bare feet protruding beneath colourful skirts. She had no intention of being tamed, but perhaps her passion was gradually mellowing. Yes, she might now consider sharing her life again and allowing closer relationships to be formed.

Since leaving England, Marina had travelled around Europe aimlessly. Her parents had left a substantial bequest and, after finally purchasing a small Cornish cottage by the sea, she had left the safe shores of her homeland and travelled to France. Still feeling restless, she explored further, finally passing through Switzerland into Italy.

Marina had heard many tales of the beauty of Tuscany and particularly the stunning mountain villages in the Apennines above Lucca. She decided that she would like to rent a modest house in Tereglio or Montefegatesi.

Chapter Two

Marina arrived in the Spa town of Bagni de Lucca on a hot afternoon in August. She parked in the town square and went in search of a hotel to spend the first few days of her stay and to use as a base to search for a suitable property.

She needed to cool down following the long drive from Pisa and, after enquiring at a local bar over a chilled beer and delicious *panini*, walked up the slope to the charming oasis of the local pool.

Glistening turquoise, bathed in the late afternoon sun, she jumped into the inviting soft water and relished the pure sensation of complete immersion in its rippling depths.

It was during this beautiful moment that she encountered him. Ruggiero was a friend of the *bagnino*; the ebullient lifeguard in charge of the pools, who had a gaudy pet macaw called Giga.

The squawking bird, balanced on top of a bright red director-style chair, attracted an audience of inquisitive swimmers. Some whistled or called 'Ciao', which he imitated, head turned from side to side, clawing at the material of his shaky perch.

At first, she ignored the Italian's gentle advances, as he tentatively asked her name. Eventually, realising he was just being friendly, she responded and they spent the next few hours diving into the pool using the two raised springboards. He showed off his back dive and Marina executed a perfect swallow dive, to exclamations of 'Bravo and Encora' from excited onlookers.

As the evening shadows began to lengthen, Marina returned to the albergo alone, feeling refreshed and ready for a good meal.

She had agreed to meet Ruggiero later at a popular restaurant near the Devil's Bridge, just outside the town in Borgo a Mozzano.

The bridge was famous in the area, with mysterious tales of witches, devils and characters of local folklore. The ancient stone structure arched in a dramatic peak at the centre of the main section, with smaller arches on either side.

Evidently, before the installation of the huge dam that spanned the river Serchio, the water level was much lower. Therefore, the drop would have been even more extreme.

Ruggiero had described the bridge and its medieval history to her and the fact that it had even survived the Nazi bombing during the Second World War, but nothing prepared her for the real encounter. These awe-inspiring bridges were miraculous in medieval times with their gravity-defying structures.

His description, in rather broken English, went as follows:

'So why rename the Ponte della Maddalena to Ponte del Diavolo, because of the devil, of course. The man appointed to build the bridge despaired at being unable to finish his job on time. So Lucifer approached him and offered to assist. The man was deeply grateful, and couldn't believe his luck. But of course, there was a price to pay. "The first soul who crosses the bridge will be mine," said the devil, ready with the contract to sign. The stonemason consented. After all, what was a single soul in exchange for a bridge that would bring wealth and commerce to the town?

'It took a single night for the unholy creature to complete this majestic bridge over the River Serchio. The following morning, when the man saw the imposing bridge reflected in the water, he finally realised what he had done. He ran to his confessor and told him everything. "Don't despair," said the priest. "We'll send a dog to cross the bridge before anyone else." The devil, outwitted and scorned, disappeared into the Serchio, never to be seen again.

'It is said that the dog, a white Maremma sheepdog, is sometimes seen walking on the bridge in the evenings at the end of October, and that he is the devil still looking for the soul of the head construction worker'.

Marina's musings were interrupted by the arrival of Ruggiero in his quaint old Cinquecento, tomato-red, with shiny chrome bumpers. The open-top material roof was folded back and he waved his greeting through the space above. He had brown slim but muscular arms and expressive hands.

"Ciao, Marina," he called, "meet my special amico," he said with a wry grin. "This is Luigi."

Marina smiled back warmly, as he indicated the little car with its number plate from Lucca, which started with the letters 'LU'.

He had drawn up next to her own car, which was a black Mini in a shiny modern version. The two cars were a juxtaposition of very different eras.

Before the meal, Ruggiero suggested that they walk across the bridge. Marina looked down on the dimly-lit rocky river bed below. Ruggiero touched her arm gently and she was once again woken from her reverie.

His English was fairly fluent as he had studied at school and continued conversation lessons through his father's olive oil business, to enable him to communicate with international clients.

He explained to Marina that during the winter months, the river could turn into a raging torrent and was sometimes very dangerous. They stood on the bridge watching for falling stars in the quiet of the evening.

After a delicious dinner of *antipasta* and spicy sausages with potatoes and green beans, they parted by their cars. Ruggiero held her briefly in his arms and asked if she would meet him the next evening. He would take her to Tereglio for the annual summer festival. "A domaini," he called, as he headed off.

"A domani," she echoed in response.

Marina felt elated but confused by how quickly she had become so close to this handsome Italian. There was something irresistible about his mixture of warm intelligence and light-hearted conversation. She had observed the marked contrast between her grey-green eyes and pale golden skin and his dark brown eyes, set deeply into the chestnut-coloured complexion.

Her last close relationship had been with a young Irishman. Connor was a musician who Marina had met in Waterford, whilst staying with friends. He had been performing with a cèilidh band in The Green Shamrock, a pub famous for its folk music and velvety Guinness, the foam decorated with shamrock shapes by the garrulous bar staff.

As she watched his nimble fingers flying up and down the fingerboard and the bow rhythmically drawn over the strings of his fiddle, in perfect time to the 'bodhrán', she was captivated. He had looked up and winked cheekily, full of Gaelic charm, and they were soon sharing stories at the bar as the last customers left.

Their romance had been short-lived, as although they had been matched in a passion for life, she was unsure about his lack of direction. Marina told him of her plans to settle in France or Italy, but he seemed happy to continue touring around the pubs and clubs of Ireland with no ambition to travel. Connor tried to persuade her to stay longer—his bright blue eyes sought hers with a longing expression and he wrapped his strong arms around her slim shoulders—but she had already made her decision.

"I have to go, Connor," she had explained. "There is so much I want to experience, so I have to move on. I do care for you so much, but it's not enough…" Marina's voice trailed off as she saw his hurt expression. "I am so sorry," she'd said, as she loosened his embrace and moved towards the door.

"Call me when you return."

"I will," she had whispered, as she closed the creaking door behind her.

Chapter Three

The next morning, Marina set off up the hills towards the picturesque village of Tereglio. The chestnut trees lining the twisting narrow road were already showing their spiny green cases and the sky was a sparkling blue in the brilliant morning sunlight.

It took about twenty minutes for her to wend her way up the hillside, encountering numerous tricky S bends, as the grey ribbon-like road snaked its course to the spine at the top, where the village straddled the hillside, with moss-covered stone houses and terracotta tiled roofs.

As Marina negotiated the steep ascent, she passed an abandoned villa set in the recess of the cliffs by the mountain road. In its day, the villa must have been a grandiose building of extraordinary beauty, nestled in this precarious position overlooking the stunning valley, many metres below.

This place captured her imagination at once, despite the open frames of the numerous empty windows, which stared out, like the stony gaze of a coma victim.

Marina stopped in a layby and walked back to the ruin. It would be a massive project to restore the decaying grandeur, but she was mesmerized and a determined glint appeared in her eyes, which to anyone who knew her well, was the prelude to a new phase, which she would see to the bitter end. Marina had trained as a designer and she enjoyed a challenge.

Tereglio was as charming and unspoilt as she had imagined. Entering through the main archway into the village, she parked her car in a small square and then wandered down one of the cobbled streets. She passed a bakery that emitted aromas of freshly baked bread and continued down to the church.

Marina felt so relaxed and happy. The smiling faces of the locals and the stunning views across the valleys filled her with *dolce vita*. She decided to spend the day here and explore the village.

As the shadows lengthened, Marina made her way down to the open space below, where awnings had been pitched for the evening festivities.

There were trestle tables covered in brightly checked red tablecloths and food was being prepared by some of the local women. They beckoned her over and a man running the bar offered her a cold beer. Ruggiero had planned to meet her there and she was relieved to see him approaching her, smiling, with a small bouquet of wild flowers. "How beautiful," she cried. "I'm so happy to see you."

Fairy lights had been strung between the trees and they added a magical quality to the celebrations. The evening was perfect and, as they danced to music from a band, they became closer and shared a wonderful intimacy in the unique surroundings of the medieval village.

The next morning, Marina awoke in a dream; she couldn't remember how the evening had ended and then, she sensed his warm body beside her. Now she recalled, he had driven her back to the town, as she had been so tired and had fallen asleep on the way back. He had helped her into her room and she had offered for him to stay.

As he began to stir, she observed his long eyelashes and youthful face, and she felt a warmth towards him that she believed he shared.

There was no awkwardness between them and he said that he wanted to spend Sunday showing her a local beauty spot. "Bring your swimsuit," he said. "I'll get one of the locals to bring your car back later."

Ruggerio took Marina to a hidden place upriver from Bagni di Lucca. They parked beside the road under some trees for shelter from the searing heat, and scrambled down the stony path. Suddenly a blue-green pool was revealed below them, the deep water, glassy clear, glinting in the sunlight. Tiny fish darted beneath the surface and the ripples circled in small eddies.

Laughing happily, they quickly discarded their clothes, which lay strewn on the warm smooth boulders. They jumped quickly into the freezing cold river water, as it gurgled down over the rocks and through narrow gullies. A rope swing hung down from an overhanging branch, so Ruggiero showed Marina how to clamber up, swing out widely, and then jump into the deep pool below.

It was a memorable day; she forgot all her plans for the future and just allowed herself to be immersed in nature. They lay back on the warm, smooth boulders, soaking up the late afternoon sun of golden hour, marvelling at the small brown lizards with vivid yellow markings, darting between the rocks.

After resting for some time, Marina slowly stood up and looked down at the inviting water; she wanted to feel the cool ripple against her warm skin again. Glancing down at the sleeping figure beside her, she decided not to disturb him, so scrambled down to the river alone.

Most of the locals had left, so it was very quiet, apart from the buzzing of insects hidden in the undergrowth and an occasional rustle of birds. She had the chance to think and, as Marina lowered her dusty feet into the green-tinted depths, her mind was full of questions: 'Why am I here? What am I doing? Am I making the right decisions?'

Just at that moment, she felt the soft touch of his hand on her shoulder, "Are you happy, Marina," he asked quietly. Ruggiero had woken and seen her looking pensive, staring into the glistening pools and had moved down to join her.

She turned and looked deep into his eyes, a slight tightening of her brows showing the mental struggle.

"Yes, I think so, but I'm still trying to get used to that feeling of accepting permanence in one place, however enchanting it is. I've been in turmoil for so long and finally, I believe I have found a place to build a new life, it's just quite daunting."

Ruggiero smiled at her reassuringly, his eyes revealing a true empathy for her struggle. "I do understand how you feel. I too have experienced this and it took me some time to accept that I was ready to find some stability, but what better place than this?" he exclaimed, opening his arms out wide to indicate the beautiful scene before them.

Marina smiled warmly, feeling energized by his enthusiastic proclamation. He was right, she would be missing an incredible experience if she failed to embrace all of this and to share it with such a man, possibly her soulmate. It all seemed unreal, but following the untimely death of her parents in a car accident some years ago, she had been like a boat without a rudder, being swept by the tides without finding a true purpose.

Perhaps this was the opening chapter of her *rinascimento*.

Chapter Four

The next morning, Marina awoke with a new purpose and drive. Many of the doubts which had clouded her mind the day before had dispersed, like the glistening mist evaporating with the sun's warm rays on the mountain peaks.

Once again, the vision she had formed in her head of resurrecting the abandoned villa on the hill road, became more real. Marina believed it would make a wonderful place for a restaurant with live music, a haunt for local creative people and many of the hordes of tourists who visited Tuscany.

She was hoping that Ruggiero would be able to connect her with artisans in the area who could restore the crumbling building to its former glory. She had no real experience of such a huge project, but the task was a challenge and this felt like the right time to take a leap of faith, so to speak.

This thought suddenly transported her back to the Devil's Bridge and a shiver ran down her spine. Marina was not naturally superstitious, but there was something about the tale that Ruggiero had expressed in such an eloquent way, despite his faltering English, which had struck deeply into her psyche. Already a name for the new restaurant had formed in her mind, *La Caduta di Lucifero*, The Fall of Lucifer. She remembered stories from her grandfather, who had been the vicar of a small parish in a Cornish village. He had told her the story of Lucifer, the fallen angel from the Bible, recorded so dramatically in the book of Ezekiel in the Old Testament.

Marina had researched the story of Lucifer in detail, after the visit to the bridge with Ruggiero and the words of that vivid biblical tale still haunted her dreams. It was almost as if the guiding hand of another being was drawing her into a different world.

She dressed quickly and left the *albergo* to find breakfast in a local café. Ruggiero was away on business and she had the whole day to herself to explore the area. Her first plan was to visit the deserted villa and make some sketches of how it could be restored. She was not an expert, but her university degree in design had given her a strong base for understanding structures and forming ideas. The villa looked less foreboding in the crisp morning light and she felt optimistic and energized. There were beautiful fragrant creepers woven around the stone arches framing those blank-eyed window frames and she recognized them as bougainvillea and the sweet perfume of white jasmine. There was also an ancient wisteria, or *glicine*, as it was known locally, clinging to the broken walls, the late purple blooms cascading over the mossy edges and thick gnarled boughs digging into the craggy stonework.

She stooped under the vines and found herself in what would have been a large impressive hallway; there were still remnants of the opulent beauty that had clothed this elegant building. She imagined the sound of guests arriving from those times and could almost hear the clatter of horses' hooves as carriages drew up outside, the rustle of sweeping gowns and the murmur of greetings.

A sweeping staircase led to the upper floor, the spindles of the banisters leaning out precariously like broken teeth. As she continued to explore the next room, a bird nesting in an alcove was disturbed and suddenly rose into the pungent air and swept past her head. Feeling unnerved, Marina decided to return another time with Ruggiero, as it was probably unsafe to penetrate further into the other rooms, which were crumbling and derelict.

Stepping back out into the bright sunshine, she realised that she had been transported back into earlier times, which once again triggered her curiosity. There must be some archive in the nearest town where she could research this villa and find out more about the previous occupants.

Marina had arranged to speak to the agent who was selling the property later that day, so she would make enquiries in Bagni di Lucca and see if she could find a local historian. Her Italian was not fluent, but she had a good understanding of the language.

What had started as a modest project was now unfolding into a massive one, which would completely possess her whole being.

She drove back to her lodgings in an old Fiat Cinquecento which Ruggiero had found for her; it was a good idea of his to return the hire car, now that she had decided to stay indefinitely. It was wonderful to feel the breeze in her hair and the pungent smell of wild herbs, as she negotiated the sharp bends of the mountain road. The views were spectacular and her spirits rose, as she thought of the evening ahead with Ruggiero. They had arranged to meet at the restaurant near the Devil's Bridge, where they enjoyed their first evening together.

Chapter Five

"I have something important I need to tell you," he said, looking deep into her eyes. "Now that we are sharing so much of our future plans, it's important that you know more about me."

Marina interrupted him. "Wait, I too have more to explain about my family, but you go first." She felt anxious and a real sense of foreboding, why did he look so worried? She had never really observed the creases on his forehead that revealed the tension in his handsome face.

"I wanted to tell you before, but now it is essential that you know, as he has turned up at my apartment."

"Who are you talking about?" she asked, curious to know what was bothering him.

"Giovanni, my brother, but he is also my twin."

Marina was shocked, as this was the first time, he had mentioned him. "Well, that's a surprise," she exclaimed, laughing a little nervously. Ruggiero seemed agitated and was fidgeting with the napkin on the table, in their favourite corner of the restaurant. "Why is it a problem, what's he like?"

"To be honest, Giovanni is a complete nightmare, he is dishonest and a waste of space. He's always asking the family to bail him out of one financial mess or another. I think he gambles, as my father has been giving him a generous allowance for years, since he dropped out of his studies in Firenze."

"What was he studying?" Marina was curious about this brother, who seemed the complete opposite of this man whom she had become so close to.

"Business studies, but he is so lazy and spent the whole time drinking and going to parties. Gio has no head for numbers, so I don't know why my father bothered. He would have been better staying here and learning more about the olive oil business, but he drove everyone crazy with his antics. I was hoping that we would spend more time together before he surfaced and started to interfere."

"Actually, since we are discussing our families, I also need to warn you about mine." Marina's face reddened.

Now it was Ruggiero's turn to look surprised. "But I thought you lost your parents many years ago in the fatal car accident."

"Yes, that's true, but I have an older sister called Cassandra, who I have never mentioned and that is because we are estranged."

A waiter came to enquire if they wanted more wine but Ruggiero waved him away. "Al momento, no, grazie." He was intrigued by Marina's admission, as she had described herself as an orphan and he had assumed she had no siblings.

She continued. "I can sympathise with you, Ruggiero, as my sister has caused me nothing but stress, I do feel sorry for her as she was diagnosed with bipolar a few years ago, when she had to be sectioned, but she can be so cruel and her mood swings are impossible to manage. If you met her, she would try to charm you and appear innocent, but she is always planning something and is intensely jealous of me. Cassandra thinks that I was my father's favourite, but it's not true. My mother spoiled her, as she thought she would never have children until Cassie came along, so having her was a gift. However, she had really bad post-natal depression and always felt guilty, as she believed this triggered Cassie's mental instability."

Marina suddenly felt so relieved that she was able to share this secret with him. She now realized that she must be deeply in love to open up in this way.

"What a pair we are!" he suddenly exclaimed, raising his arms in a futile gesture, and both of them couldn't help suppressing their laughter.

"Yes," she said, her shoulders shaking by now, as she tried to control herself. "Demanding siblings, but with any luck you won't have to meet mine."

Ruggiero grinned wryly. "Unfortunately, you might, if you are willing to brave a family dinner at my parents' villa. They have invited us to dine together on Friday evening, can you bear it?" he asked, with a pained expression. "My mama keeps pestering me about who the mysterious girl is that I am dating. Some locals have seen us together, so it is no longer a secret, sorry about that."

"It's not a problem Ruggiero, I'd love to come and I'm sure that I can handle your brother, he can't be as difficult as my sister."

"You wait!" Ruggiero exclaimed.

They left the restaurant soon after this intense exchange and wandered across the ancient bridge in the eerie light of a waning silver moon. Owls were calling in the night and leaves were rustling in a gentle breeze. Marina felt much closer to him, now that they had shared their secrets, but she still had an uneasy feeling, as though her present happy state was about to be shattered.

Chapter Six

The next morning was clear and bright with a brisk wind, which made the feathery clouds scud across the cerulean sky. Once again, Marina was in awe of this beautiful place, despite her misgivings the previous day.

Ruggiero had planned to collect her for a beach day near Pisa. She was excited about a change of scene and this seemed like the perfect time.

As they drove to Marina di Vecchiano, Ruggiero discussed the history of the coastal area with her. He became more animated, as he proudly explained that Pisa was not far from the sea and that during its golden age, from the eleventh to the thirteenth centuries, the city was one of the maritime powers of the Mediterranean. She marvelled at his enthusiasm and enjoyed watching his distinctive profile and strong jawline. Sometimes his hand rested gently on her knee, in between gestures at the unfolding landscape, and she allowed herself to daydream a little, as the wind ruffled her long hair through the open sun roof.

The beach was fairly deserted as they had arrived early, but it was already becoming quite hot and there was no shelter on the beach. Ruggiero started to collect driftwood that was strewn in piles on the warm sand and she suddenly realized that he was creating a structure to shield them from the sun. She joined in and they began to search for just the right pieces to make it secure. Marina began to feel like a wild thing; she was carefree like the seagulls that were soaring high above, calling with abandon. They laughed together and threw themselves down on colourful towels beneath the bleached branches.

The salty air smelt fresh and the sea glittered invitingly as it lapped on the shoreline. Marina was just about to change into her swimming costume, when Ruggiero suddenly tensed and looked anxious. She could see a distant figure heading towards them and she felt uneasy. "I don't believe it," he exclaimed. "It's Gio!"

"How did he know we were here?" Marina responded.

"My parents must have told him that we were going to the coast and he knows this is one of my special places. I just can't understand why he has to come and spoil everything."

By now, Giovanni was approaching rapidly and Marina was shocked by the similarity of the brothers. They were not identical twins but the resemblance was still uncanny. However, as he drew even closer, she observed a downward turn to the corners of his mouth and a slightly arrogant expression in his eyes.

Giovanni looked her up and down and she felt uncomfortable. "Thanks for inviting me to your little party," he said sarcastically, "Aren't you going to introduce me, brother?"

Ruggiero looked furious and glared at him, "You're not welcome here, Gio. Marina and I wanted a peaceful day alone, without unwelcome visitors."

"Oh, come on, let's be friendly and forget past differences. It's been so long since we spent time together and I would love to get to know your new girlfriend." He said this looking pointedly at Marina and giving her a coy look.

She felt awkward and could sense the real animosity between the brothers. Marina sympathised with Ruggiero but she didn't want to spoil the day. "I'm going for a swim, so can you both give me some space while I change." She was determined not to get involved and the young men moved away while she slipped into the swimsuit which she had bought recently. The bright red material was striking in the intense sunlight and she felt the admiring glances of the brothers, who turned for a moment from their heated conversation. "Come on, you two, let's just enjoy ourselves," she called, trying to lighten the atmosphere.

Ruggiero's expression was so angry that Marina thought he was going to explode, so she tried to give him a reassuring look, as they walked back towards her. She examined the face of the brother more closely and had to admit that there was something very unsavoury about his whole manner, which was reflected in the frown marks on his bronzed forehead. Marina remembered observing Ruggiero in the restaurant the night before, when he was concerned during their discussion about their siblings, but his face had revealed an open and trustworthy appearance.

She decided she should make an effort, despite this uncomfortable situation. Marina held out her hand. "Hello, good to meet you."

It was a vain attempt at friendliness, as Giovanni was obviously aware that she had been warned of his character. However, he also broke the tension by responding almost too warmly, "Piacere mio, naturalmente, cara Marina, you understand a little Italian?" he enquired with a smile.

"Some," she responded, as Ruggiero glared at his brother's over familiar manner.

"Enough of introductions," he said abruptly. "Are we going swimming or not, now you're here."

The brothers threw off their clothes and they all ran towards the glistening water. The sand was hot beneath their feet, so it was a relief to dive into the rippling waves and feel the cool water lapping around their bodies. Marina stayed close to her partner, but Giovani struck out into the deeper water, showing off his powerful front crawl as he cut through the waves. It was a relief to be alone again and she stroked his head gently, trying to reassure him, that she understood and empathised. Ruggiero was still upset by his brother's interference, but he didn't want to create a bad atmosphere and decided to pretend nothing had happened as they floated on their backs, fingers entwined.

As it was time to eat, Ruggiero swam back to the beach to start a fire, so they could barbecue some of the seafood he had packed for their lunch. Marina continued to float in the swell of the gentle waves and felt peaceful. There was no sign of his brother, so she had begun to relax and forget the earlier unpleasantness.

Suddenly, she felt a searing pain in her legs as something brushed past her; it was a burning sensation and she struggled in the water. She had floated out quite deep by now. Marina cried out and then Giovanni suddenly appeared from nowhere.

"Calmati, starai bene… There are jellyfish." He put his arms around her and managed to support her on the surface of the water. Despite her initial fear, his reassuring words calmed her, but she was crying from the stabbing sensation in her limbs. By now, Ruggiero was on the scene and he rushed in to help, lifting her up and transporting her to the fire which he had built near their shelter.

"Are you all right, is it still hurting?" She was too shocked to answer properly and just nodded her head. "Get some ice out of the cool bag, Gio, and put it on her legs," he instructed his brother. His brother reacted quickly and then he asked for Marina's bag, as Ruggiero knew she carried antihistamine, which would relieve any swelling. She looked so vulnerable lying there and he felt responsible for this. He should have warned her, as there were often shoals of small jellyfish which could multiply considerably, if the sea was particularly warm.

Giovanni was observing them both, but was looking more intently at Marina. He seemed very moved by her situation which annoyed Ruggiero. He always seemed to be around when there was a crisis, but he realised on this occasion he was probably being unfair. All he wanted, was for his brother just to leave them be, especially as his main consideration was just to tend to Marina. He reached for a towel and put it around her quivering shoulders. She was looking quite pale and he decided they should head back as soon as possible. So much for the perfect day he had planned for them.

"I can handle this now, thanks. You can go back home."

His brother had a hurt expression. "I want to help her too."

"Well, I don't need you to assist, so please just go."

Giovanni began to protest, but seeing the pleading look in Marina's face, he gave way and turned to go. "I'm so sorry, Marina, I hope you recover quickly."

She murmured her thanks to his retreating figure and, despite her anguish, she suddenly felt some warmth towards him for his quick action and compassion. Maybe he wasn't so bad, she thought.

Ruggiero continued to make her feel comfortable. He gave her a glass of wine to steady her nerves and then doused the fire, so they could leave quickly. She suddenly felt a flood of tiredness sweep over her, she couldn't wait to get into his car and drift off to sleep.

On the journey back they hardly spoke, as Marina was drifting in an out of consciousness. As she slept, visions appeared in her head of the Devil's Bridge, Lucifer crashing to the rocky riverbed below and shady figures floating in the gloom.

"Wake up, Marina, you're dreaming." Ruggiero's voice suddenly broke through the vision and he sounded so concerned. She had been moaning in her sleep. "Do you want me to pull over for a few minutes and get some coffee?"

"No, no, I'm fine, I just want to get back to the albergo."

"I don't think that's a good idea, Marina. I'll take you back to my parent's villa and we will call out the medico locale, if necessary, to check on you."

She was too exhausted to argue and fell back into a reverie, but this time she felt more relaxed, as she allowed Ruggiero to take care of her.

As they pulled into the drive of the Villa Giannini, Marina was first aware of the sound of deep gravel beneath the wheels of the car. She lifted her head and looking up through the sunroof she saw a thick mass of dark green foliage from the surrounding pine trees. She felt apprehensive, as she realized how grand the whole estate appeared, looking back down the long avenue wending its way to the main gated entrance. It was lined with the pointed Tuscan cypress trees so characteristic of the area, with their slender and distinctive shape.

Ruggiero was aware that she must be feeling anxious and he spoke quietly. "Marina, they will love you. My parents are very open and I have told them how happy you have made me over these past few weeks" She sighed loudly and he clasped her hand reassuringly. "I'm fine. I'm still a little in shock after the incident in the water, my skin feels so uncomfortable."

"Don't worry, darling, my mama is used to dealing with all sorts of ailments, bringing up two sons."

"Is your brother going to be here?" She was worried about another difficult encounter.

"I doubt it, he usually stays out until later, otherwise he gets into arguments when he is bored of hanging around the house."

"That's a relief," she said, as she smiled warmly and lifted herself up fully in the car seat.

"Are you ready to meet them, Marina?"

"I think so." She was still feeling unsure, but then realised that this was an important occasion for him, as he said he rarely introduced girlfriends to his family. 'I can do this,' she said to herself.

His mother was as warm and welcoming as Ruggiero had described. Sophia appeared suddenly and rushed over to the car. She was concerned about Marina, as her son had phoned beforehand from the beach to explain what had happened. "Mio caro, per favore, vieni con me, posso prenderti il braccio." Her face was open and friendly.

Marina felt overwhelmed but she was grateful for the support. "Grazie, si." she tried to sound confident.

She was guided up the marble stairs to the main entrance. As they entered the hallway, she saw an imposing figure standing before her. He had piercing eyes and seemed to be assessing her as she leaned on Sophia's arm.

"Danilo, are you just going to stand there? Come and greet Ruggiero's friend," his wife ordered in perfect English, with a strong assertive accent

Suddenly the face that had appeared so stern changed like a sunbeam breaking through heavy clouds.

"Of course, I am very sorry," he attempted in broken English. "You are so welcome."

Marina suddenly felt faint and Ruggiero was just in time to catch her, as she swayed to one side.

"You, poor child," Sophia declared.

"Take Marina to the guest room to rest and we will talk later."

Marina accepted gratefully and Ruggiero helped her to climb the polished wooden staircase to the first floor.

All she could remember after that, was sinking into a wonderful bed with soft covers and falling into a deep sleep.

Chapter Seven

Marina began to dream. She was transported back to her youth and images of her parents and sister appeared. It seemed so real and she could remember every detail.

She was walking along a path by the cliff that overlooked one of their favourite Cornish beaches. It was a Sunday, as they liked to enjoy some fresh air after the church service, before having an afternoon meal, usually a roast. In this dream, Marina was clinging to her father's arm and trying to console him and she remembered it had been something about her sister.

It all came flooding back, years of anguish and disruption. Cassandra, with her mane of dark hair, cold blue eyes and unpredictable nature. Their poor father, a quiet country vicar of a small parish and their mother, the daughter of local gentry, working as a teacher in the village school.

Cassandra always had to be the centre of attention; the symptoms of her mental illness were not diagnosed fully until her early twenties. Their parents did not want to believe it and thought it was just a stage in her development. However, it all made sense when they finally accepted the diagnosis of bipolar from a psychiatrist, on referral to the nearest specialist clinic.

Everything had come to a head, when the couple were preparing for a well-deserved holiday. It was just after Easter, and they had decided to take a short walking vacation in Scotland. Her father's brother lived in Dundee and was always asking them to visit.

Marina's mother was finishing the final packing and her father was checking the car, when Cassandra had suddenly appeared unexpectedly. She was brandishing a hammer and looking deranged. She approached the car and suddenly started striking a tyre in a frenzied attack. Marina remembered the look of disbelief on her father's face, as they watched from the kitchen window.

"What on earth are you doing, Cassie?" he was shouting.

"You don't deserve a holiday," she screamed. "I never have holidays. Why are you going off without me? I'm the one who needs a break. You're so selfish, it's not fair," she sobbed.

"Calm down," he said, but she was totally out of control and dropping the hammer, she struck him on the face, breaking his glasses and pushing him aside.

"Lock the door, Ruth," he called out to his wife, "she's out of control."

"Should I call the police?" she said to Marina in a fluster,

"No, no, I'll deal with her," she replied as steadily as she could.

Marina recalled calming her sister down and persuading her to visit the local hospital to speak to one of the psychiatrists there. It wasn't the first time there had been an outburst, but never as bad, and she had obviously stopped taking her medication.

Cassandra was sectioned in a voluntary capacity, after the careful persuasion of specialist doctors, as they were concerned for the safety of her family, and to prevent any self-harm.

It was horrible to be a witness to this, but Marina knew it was the right course of action.

That was the first of many episodes and it seemed so real, that when Ruggiero came in to wake her for dinner, Marina was sure she was still in her parent's home, comforting her mother.

She felt disorientated and her whole being filled like a darkened well, with sorrow and recriminations. She often wondered if her sister's mental health issues had been managed much earlier, then maybe their parents could still be alive now.

But what was the point, nothing could be altered, only the present and the future.

She had no idea where her sister was living now, as they had been out of contact for many years. Marina was not sure she wanted to reopen the wounds which still haunted her to this day; she was sure that Cassandra would still be in denial and refusing help and medication.

Ruggiero was speaking to her again, so she banished the nightmares and listened to his comforting tones.

"Marina, you need to eat, let's go down."

"I can't yet, I'm still shaky and I don't feel like eating. Please can I meet your parents properly tomorrow?"

"Of course, non problema, cara." He withdrew quietly and left her to rest. It had been a strange and eventful day and he felt confused and unsettled.

Ruggiero was determined to think positively and he descended to the dining room to have dinner with his parents. As he entered the candlelit room, he could see the concern on their faces.

He reassured them that she was feeling much better, but just needed to rest and recuperate until the next day.

They sat down to their meal and despite still feeling sorry for Marina, he was so hungry that he began to enjoy the steaming bowl of spaghetti alla vongele, which was one of his favourites. The sauce was delicious and he wiped the drops from his mouth with a crisp white serviette, as he reached for more olive ciabbata.

The conversation at the table was relaxed and friendly, as Ruggiero had a close relationship with them both. He knew his parents tried to treat their sons equally, but years of contention had broken down their trust of his twin.

He could see the strain around his mother's eyes and the furrows in his father's forehead, which were not just signs of ageing but the stress and strain of dealing with a wayward son.

Ruggiero did not rejoice in his own virtues, as he was by no means perfect, and he had tried for many years to be close with his brother. In the end, after many extreme episodes, including a fight, when he had tried to defend his brother from some angry creditor, he realised that his efforts were futile and Giovanni would either change or continue in a downward spiral which could eventually be fatal.

As they moved onto the dessert of tiramasu, a coffee flavoured sponge with mascarpone and dusted with chocolate, he mused on the name, 'pick me up' or 'cheer me up'. It seemed as if his mother had thought of this ahead and they smiled at each other; her eyes had a mischievous glint and she looked like her old positive self, the playful companion of his childhood.

Even his father appeared more cheerful and they teased each other with stories of their past, such as when his papa had put diesel into his car instead of petrol.

He had been on his way home from an awards evening for olive oil producers and being tired, his concentration lapsed. It had been a family joke for years, as normally his father was fastidious about everything he did.

"Papa sciocco," Ruggiero gently mocked and in response, Danilo recounted the tale about Ruggiero using his air rifle while he was away some years ago and jamming the mechanism.

The boy had been so concerned about his father finding out, that he had buried the rifle in some woods at the bottom of the extensive gardens.

It was only recently that the wooden stock had been uncovered by one of the groundsmen, the barrel of the gun stuck deeply into the earth. Of course, Ruggiero had to come clean and his father had laughed and stated that he often wondered where that rifle had disappeared.

They laughed heartily while his mother slipped away to speak to the kitchen staff before calling goodnight to them, as she wanted to continue reading a book she was engrossed in before going to sleep.

The red wine began to flow and the evening ended without any mention of the events of the day. It was a time for them to reaffirm their strong bonds and enjoy some time together without the troublesome Giovanni, who had obviously decided to spend his evening in town with his depraved friends.

Chapter Eight

Marina woke early, as she could hear the dawn chorus from her room overlooking the rose garden. The sky was streaked with deep pink and orange hues and the sun was rising over the numerous trees lining the lawns.

A pair of magpies were strutting across the dew-laden grass, searching for insects. Their plumage was glossy black with a metallic green and violet sheen, which appeared to glow in the golden morning light.

She had slept well and the unwelcome dreams had banished, as she had drifted into a deep untroubled sleep due to extreme fatigue.

Marina moved across the room to the long windows and discovered that they opened out onto a Juliet balcony. It brought back memories of studying Shakespeare at school when she was about fifteen.

Yes, she remembered, the Montagues and the Capulets. She always got mixed up with which was which… She was sure Romeo was a Montague and Juliet a Capulet.

She imagined Ruggiero appearing below and calling to her…

"But, soft! what light through yonder window breaks?

It is the east, and Juliet is the sun…"

"O Romeo, Romeo! wherefore art thou Romeo
Deny thy father and refuse thy name;

Or, if thou wilt not, be but sworn my love,

And I'll no longer be a Capulet."

She then started humming a melody in her head, what was it, she thought. *Love Story* by Taylor Swift, she was obsessed with that song when it first came out, she even had it on repeat on her car CD autochanger. She sang the words softly,

Suddenly Marina felt warm arms being clasped around her and she gasped in surprise,

"Don't be frightened, it is only me."

Thinking it was Ruggiero, she turned around, only to find she was staring into the face of his dishevelled brother.

She was about to scream, but he stopped her with his hand.

"Sorry, I mean you no harm… really."

"Just get out, or I will call for Ruggiero." She was furious and a little scared, but she didn't want him to see this. "How dare you come into my room and invade my privacy. You're still drunk, look at the state you're in."

Giovanni looked sheepish now and rather ashamed. He had never met such a strong-minded woman who could speak so plainly to him.

"Sorry again, I will go. Please don't say anything to him, it will be our little secret."

Marina didn't like the conspiratorial manner in which he made this request, she just inclined her head and indicated the door. "Go now, before I change my mind," she hissed angrily, and he disappeared, silently closing the bedroom door.

She leant heavily against the wall, gasping with anxiety; she had mixed feelings of anger but also a strange feeling of excitement too. What was wrong with her? She believed that she was in love with Ruggiero, so why did she feel anything for his impudent brother, who seemed to have no respect for anything or anyone.

Marina was very shaken by this encounter but decided not to mention anything to Ruggiero, as there would only be another unpleasant scene.

However, she was unaware that their mother had also risen early, disturbed by the sound of her son closing the front door. Sophia had peered out of her door just as Giovanni entered the guest room and she guessed he was up to his old tricks. There had always been rivalry between the two boys and especially over girls, but this was really overstepping the mark.

She expected to hear Marina cry out but there was no sound and she saw her son leave some moments later looking contrite, but with a slight smile playing on his worn face. Giovanni did not see his mother as he mounted the stairs to his room on the second floor and like Marina, she thought it better not to mention this encounter either.

Perhaps when she became better acquainted with her, she might be able to advise Marina on how to handle Giovanni, but that would depend on how established this new relationship with Ruggiero would become, over the next few months.

Sophia often wondered where she had gone wrong with Gio. He had always been a difficult child, demanding and dissatisfied. She had done her best to treat the two boys equally and they had both had the advantages of a privileged life, excellent education and a close extended family.

Sophia's mother had lived with them after she was widowed and she had possibly indulged Gio. He was always a charmer and his grandmother doted on him. He would visit her regularly in the converted stables where she lived very comfortably.

Gio would play card games with her for hours when he should have been studying. This is when he started his interest in gambling.

Nonna Maria had been a glamorous socialite in her prime and she had enjoyed the high life. She modelled herself on the beautiful actress, Sophia Loren, which is why her daughter was given this name. There were often gambling tables at the parties they attended. She dragged her long-suffering husband to many of these evenings, which often lasted until the early hours.

Giovanni enjoyed listening to his Nonna's stories and became enamoured by this decadent life-style.

Danilo became very frustrated by his mother in law's antics but he was not aware of how strong her influence would be on his infatuated son. She had died a few years before and Giovanni had been devastated.

Sophia decided to go downstairs and prepare some breakfast. The staff had been given the day off, so she could spend some quiet time in the kitchen going through the satisfying routines of making coffee and warming bread in the oven. She reached for her favourite red Bialeti coffee pot and the old caddy with years of rich smells emanating from the tin. Lavazza was her chosen brand and she loved opening a brand-new packet, snipping off the top of the metallic packaging and releasing the first fresh burst of its wonderful aroma.

She opened the windows wide as the sun filtered through the turquoise shutters. Sophia suddenly experienced a feeling of true contentment, as one her tortoiseshell cats appeared on the windowsill. These were the simple pleasures of life, silently observing the dexterous feline with penetrating emerald eyes, balancing on the ledge, purring loudly.

Sophia hummed a melody from an Italian opera as she moved around the kitchen. Danilo had taken her to a performance at the Teatro dell'Opera in Firenze the weekend before and it had been a wonderful experience seeing Verdi's *La Traviata*.

She was so moved by the story of the main characters, an ill-fated couple, Violetta Valéry and

Alfredo Germont. The sets were so enchanting, with the romantic backdrop of Paris.

Sophia had read that Verdi had based his opera on the real-life story of the courtesan, Marie Duplessis. She had been the most fashionable and uncontested queen of the '*horizontales*' who serviced the city's rich bourgeoisie, upper classes, artists, writers and musicians. Her life and death had inspired Verdi's work.

She must have been a remarkable woman, as she was also the subject of *La Dame Aux Camélias* by Alexandre Dumas. They had been lovers for many months and he wrote it within a year of Duplessis' death.

It was while Sophia was recalling these stories in her head, that Marina appeared in the arched entrance, looking pale but less haunted. She immediately went over and greeted her with, "Buongiorno, come stai."

"Bene, bene," Marina replied.

Sophia pulled out a chair by the rustic table and Marina sat down, carefully wrapping a pastel blue patterned silk shawl around her shoulders. She shivered a little from the fresh breeze coming through the open window.

"You are cold?" Sophia asked.

"No, I'm fine, it's such a beautiful morning and the air is so refreshing."

Marina was happy to have some time alone with Ruggiero's mother. It was an opportunity to get to know her and she seemed relaxed and amiable.

Sophia finished making the coffee and brought some to Marina in a lovely enamelled cup; the steaming brew was delicious and revived her spirits.

They sat together in companionable silence for a while and then started discussing Marina's plans for the deserted hillside villa and the name she had chosen for it. Sophia thought this might shake up the locals whose lives were steeped in folklore, but thought it was a great idea.

She offered to go with her to Bagni di Lucca later that morning to meet the estate agent or *mediatore*, as they are known. It seemed like a good idea to get some help with the complicated system and the Italian terms with which she was unfamiliar.

After having some breakfast, Marina thanked her and disappeared upstairs to have a bath. There was still no sign of any of the others, so she planned to have a long luxurious soak in the stunning ensuite marble bathroom.

Chapter Nine

Ruggiero had woken in a good mood, later that morning. The evening spent with his parents had been really positive and he was looking forward to introducing Marina to them properly.

However, when he knocked on Marina's door, he was surprised to find that there was no response. Puzzled, he descended the grand staircase and then heard an animated discussion coming from the dining room.

His parents were sitting at the table with Marina and they appeared to have already built a rapport. Even his father was grinning and looking admiringly at his girlfriend. Marina had taken extra care with her appearance and Ruggiero recognised the deep blue dress she was wearing from his mother's own wardrobe. She looked stunning and fresh faced, so different from the night before.

All the tension from yesterday was swept away and he felt excited about their future plans.

He joined them for a breakfast of hot rolls and marmellata di fragile, locally produced strawberry jam. More coffee was served and they continued their discussion about work with his father and Marina's plans for the music venue.

He was pleased to hear that his mother wanted to assist Marina with the mediatore and they made arrangements to meet his parents later in town.

Just as they were leaving, Giovanni appeared, still looking the worse for wear. Marina's face reddened as she recalled what had happened earlier. He looked at her enquiringly and she shook her head.

Ruggiero ignored his brother and holding Marina's hand, led her out into the sunlight to his car.

The journey back was perfect as Marina felt so much better and the marks on her legs had gone down completely, after the welts that had appeared on them yesterday. She would definitely be more careful of jellyfish next time they swam in the sea.

Although she liked the borrowed dress, it was rather too stylish for her taste and she was looking forward to getting back to her rented rooms and changing into casual clothes. "You look like an Italian model in that outfit," Ruggiero teased.

"Not quite, but it is a beautiful dress. I will get it cleaned later and return it to your mother."

"I wouldn't worry, she has a huge collection."

As they drove into the square where the small hotel was located, Ruggiero drew up next to the entrance and leant over to kiss Marina. He was looking forward to spending the evening alone with her, as they were not planning to return to the family villa.

"I really enjoyed meeting your parents, especially your mother. I'll meet you in an hour at the office of the agent." She realised that she was starting to use Italian phrasing with her English.

Perhaps she could become a local after all.

His parents were true to their word. Marina watched them, as Danilo came round to the passenger side of their sleek glossy black Lancia, to assist his elegant wife, who gracefully took the offered hand. She was stunning and appeared remote, but Marina had experienced her warm nature and was no longer afraid.

The mediatore started to change his rather off-hand attitude, when he realised he would be dealing with the whole Giannini family. Nothing was too much trouble, and after looking over the paperwork, an appointment was made for the late afternoon to view the villa that Marina was so excited about.

"Who's ready for lunch," Ruggiero announced. They all assented, as it was past one o'clock and it had already been a long morning for the two women, after their early unexpected encounter.

Danilo suggested a nearby restaurant owned by one of his old friends. Ristorante Sul Fiume, as its name implied, was situated by the River Lima, not far from the Ponte della Maddalena, the Devil's Bridge.

The restaurant was famous for its tasty dishes and large tables with cosy armchairs. The main interior room had a large crystal chandelier. Sophia and Danilo both had a love of desserts and particularly the famous

Chantilly cream tart with wild berries, which was delicious.

As they walked there, Danilo took Marina's arm in his own and Ruggiero followed with his mother. Marina was fascinated to learn more about the town, so Danilo recounted some history of the area.

He spoke in a gentle tone, much like that used by Ruggiero.

"Bagni di Lucca is now rather a quiet town, but one hundred and fifty years ago, it was one of the most popular and most visited destinations in Italy. As you know, the River Lima flows through the town centre, which is part of the Val di Lima.

"From the first half of the nineteenth century, royalty and nobles from across Europe flocked to the town, not just because of the therapeutic powers of the spa waters, but also because it had one of the very first casinos to open in Europe. It attracted many of the great literary and artistic figures of the nineteenth century, such as Shelley, Byron, Puccini and Browning.

"It was here in Bagni di Lucca that the game of roulette was invented almost two hundred years ago."

Marina could only just suppress a gasp of astonishment and looked away from him. She had immediately thought of Giovanni. So, she mused, gambling in the Giannini family may have dated back a couple of centuries.

Rodolfo was the loquacious host of the restaurant, welcoming them with open arms and squeezing

Marina's hand so hard, that she thought hers would break. Ruggiero laughed and she gave him a daggered look.

Lunch was as good as they had promised and by the time it came for desserts and coffee, Marina felt extremely full.

During the meal she had learnt much more about Rugggiero's parents. She knew that Sophia was a musician but had not realised that she had been a concert pianist.

Sophia Rossi, as she had been known then, was a highly acclaimed artist who had studied in Rome and at the famous Chigiana in Siena. It was there, one summer, that she had met Danilo, when he was attending the stag party of a close friend, in the medieval city.

The timing was not good, as she had already planned to take post-graduate studies abroad in London, at the Royal Academy of Music. She wanted to broaden her horizons and learn more about other cultures. Sophia was also fascinated by the English language and in particular the works of Shakespeare, as so many of the plots were set in her beloved Italy.

Danilo was disappointed at first, but they were still in their early twenties and he realised that it was an important opportunity for her.

In London, Sophia was immediately recognised for her unique talent and interpretations. She won a number of awards and gave her debut at the Purcell Room in the

South Bank Centre, which led to many other performances around the United Kingdom.

Sophia was even asked to play for the royal family at a special charity concert for children. It was a glittering event at Chiswick House and she felt honoured to receive this recognition.

Danilo was constantly in touch and even wrote letters to her expressing his admiration, as he knew how much she treasured these romantic gestures. Her landlady in Camden would shout from the bottom of the stairs, "Another letter from Italy, my dear," and Sophia would excitedly run down the stairs, exclaiming, "Thank you so much, Mrs Mayne, it must be Danilo…"

However, on one occasion it was not from him, but a letter from her mother to say that her father was gravely ill and she must come home as soon as possible. It was quick onset leukaemia and there was very little that could be done, except keep him comfortable and out of pain.

Sophia immediately contacted the academy and explained the situation and that she must cancel any other appearances. They gave her sympathetic leave and she was on the first plane to Pisa, clutching a hurriedly packed bag.

Danilo met her at the airport and she rushed into his arms almost collapsing from the stress of holding back her emotions during the journey home from England. He held her close and told her everything would be fine, but both of them knew that the illness was terminal.

On the way to the hospice, where Alberto had been taken for respite care, the couple travelled silently in the car. Danilo drew her towards him and she had leant against his shoulder, feeling comforted by his warm familiar fragrance.

Following her father's death, Sophia lost direction and decided that once she had taken her final recital diploma in London, she would return to Italy forever. She loved performing, but she believed that her mother would need emotional support, now she was a widow, and Danilo had already proposed to her. After some thought, she had accepted. Her only stipulation was that she wanted a long engagement, as they still had not spent much time together, because of her year abroad and because she was still grieving for the loss of her father.

Alberto had been a strong influence in her artistic life, as he was a larger-than-life character and one of largest landowners in that area of Tuscany.

His love of music had grown from a young age, as his family had known the Puccinis, and spent many incredible evenings at their villa in Torre del Lago, the famous composer's home. This obsession with music was then passed on to his eager young daughter and he encouraged her in her piano studies.

Having found out so much about Ruggiero's mother, Marina could see another side of her. Despite the dazzling smile, behind that, she now thought she could see the pain of unrealised ambitions from her curtailed career. Obviously, she had shared a wonderful life with her doting husband, but it must have been sad to sacrifice her dreams of touring the world as a concert pianist.

Marina thought about her own life; would she do the same? She had been alone for so long and always followed her own path without much thought of putting down roots. She glanced at Sophia again and once again felt connected, as their eyes seemed to meet in mutual understanding.

"Marina, are you daydreaming again?" Danilo asked.

"Oh yes, sorry, are we going now?" she replied, suddenly aware that everyone was looking at her.

"Well, we do have the appointment with the agent and my parents need to leave soon after that for a party near Lucca."

"Andiamo a tutti."

Chapter Ten

The visit to the deserted villa had been a success and they all agreed that its elevated position, with stunning views of the valley below, would be a great advantage. Danilo was a little more cautious about the costs and the condition of the crumbling foundations and suggested a very thorough structural survey, before Marina made her final offer.

As they left the site, Marina's eyes glistened with excitement; she felt that she had found a real purpose and direction in taking on this project. Also, she suddenly believed that she may have found the family unit she had been missing all these years. She had never really had chance to grieve the loss of her parents properly as, because of her sister's mental issues, Marina had taken on the role of principal carer and the duties of dealing with her parents' estate.

There was still a nagging doubt in her mind, created by the unstable foundations and insecurities of her teens and the uncertainty for the future, without the strong ties previously provided by her parents. It was so unfair that they had died suddenly in the accident, without preparations or plans for their daughters. The only decision they had made was life insurance, which at least relieved the financial burdens, even if the emotional side was a wasteland.

Marina realised that it was not healthy to keep reliving the whole tragedy; she needed to move on and create a fresh new chapter in her book of life.

It reminded her of a visit to Mexico she had experienced with an old school friend. They had saved up with various part time jobs and flights were bought by their respective parents, after they finished school.

It was an eye-opening trip. Mexican culture had a positive view on death and loss of family. The Day of the Dead, *Día de los Muertos*, celebrated the lives of those who had passed to the next world and would never be forgotten by their ancestors.

On this celebratory holiday in November, Mexicans would explore their traditions, feast on delicious food and decorated clay skulls in vivid, vibrant colours. Marina and her friend had been warmly welcomed by the local people they had met, as they travelled to Puebla, and joined in the celebrations. This was how she needed to relate to her grief and celebrate the living memories of her family.

Ruggiero's parents had left and the couple were alone at last. After a simple meal at a local *osteria*, they drove to their favourite place near the bridge by the river. Ruggiero took a rug out of the boot of his car and laid it on a stone bench. Although it was late summer, the evening was warm and the numerous stars shone brightly away from the artificial town lights.

They sat quietly, listening to the buzzing of cicadas hidden in the surrounding trees. It was so peaceful sitting there and talking over the events of the day. They laughed together and remembered the look on the agent's face when he understood that he was dealing with the whole Giannini family in the negotiations.

Then, Ruggerio suddenly became more serious and Marina felt apprehensive. He looked directly into her eyes and then knelt down and she was shocked to find that he was proposing to her.

"Marina, will you be mine?" he uttered sincerely. "I know we have only been together a short while, but I am certain of my feelings for you."

She was numb, and felt confused, it was all so sudden. Marina turned her head away for a few minutes as she collected her thoughts and emotions. Then moving back again to face him, she took his hand. "Ruggiero, I do care for you deeply, but I'm just not ready yet… please understand…"

He looked so wounded, that she knew she had to give him some hope.

"Give me time, darling, I will give you my answer by the end of the year."

She said this in such a loving way that he felt more positive and embraced her warmly.

Ruggiero has been carried away by everything that had happened over the past few weeks and perhaps he had been hasty, but he was absolutely sure in his mind that he wanted to spend his future with her.

They returned to the *albergo* and parted at the door, planning to meet the next evening, as Ruggiero would be away for the day on business. This would give them the breathing space that they both needed.

In her room, Marina went over to the window. Her head was spinning, as she looked at the empty street below. Ruggiero had left but she saw a figure standing in the gloom under one of the dim, street lamps, the head turned towards her. She tried to discern the features but they suddenly disappeared into the dark night.

Marina went to bed feeling uneasy and slept fitfully, until a rosy dawn appeared in the east and she eventually drifted into her dreams.

Chapter Eleven

"There is a message for you," the lady at the desk called, as Marina entered the lobby of the *albergo*. She had just returned from a local *panatteria* with some freshly made bread and cheese.

"Who left it?" she asked. "I'm sorry, I did not see, here it is."

The writing on the front was very familiar and a shudder ran down her spine. She ran up to her room to open the note in private. As she had already guessed, it was her sister, Cassandra. How on earth did she track her down, the only person who knew her location was the family lawyer. However, he was under strict instructions not to give out her address before checking with her first.

She knew how persuasive Cassandra could be. The poor man must have given in to her beguiling ways.

The writing was slanted and scrawled, which made it quite difficult to read.

Well, here I am in your precious Italy. I thought that we could spend some time together after you left so suddenly without telling me. I'll be back later. Cassie x

A rush of emotions overcame her and she gripped onto the rail of the ornate metal bed where she had collapsed. Cassandra was the last person she wanted to see, especially at this critical moment. All the old feelings of resentment bubbled up to the surface, transporting her back to her childhood.

It felt like an old scar had been reopened and the pain felt real, as images flashed into her mind. Cassandra, wild-eyed and angry, slamming doors and breaking the banister rails at the top of the stairs. Her mother looking white and strained in the morning, pretending everything was normal as she prepared breakfast in the cottage kitchen. No sign of her father, who had gone straight into his study to escape the fallout. Then Cassandra appearing out of nowhere, a smile playing around her face, acting as if nothing had happened the night before. Smarming up to them in an artificial way that made Marina's blood boil.

No, Marina was determined that her sister would not ruin the new life she had started here. How was she going to deal with this situation, she needed to think quickly before Cassandra's return. Her first thought was to contact Ruggiero, but he was working and it would be wrong to worry him.

She didn't want a scene here at the *albergo*, so decided to write a note for her sister and leave it with Anna at the front desk. Marina told her sister to meet her on the Devil's bridge at one o'clock, that way they would be in a remote place away from prying eyes. Now she was connected with the Giannini family, many of the locals were beginning to take an interest in her.

Hurriedly leaving the message, Marina headed down one of the cobbled side streets away from the main square, hoping that Cassandra was not lurking nearby. She felt like a hunted animal trying to escape from her pursuer, the streets were her hidden paths and she needed to find a safe place to wait for the next hour or so. She went into one of the small shops selling handmade gifts, beautiful wooden objects carved from gnarled olive wood, smooth polished plates and a cheeseboard, incorporating the knots and uneven texture. There was a cleverly fashioned corkscrew that she thought that Ruggiero would like and decided to buy it. This was the first present she had bought for him and she suddenly felt a ray of pleasure, despite this difficult predicament. The twinkly-eyed shopkeeper wrapped the gift in some green tissue paper and she placed it carefully in her shoulder bag.

It seemed so strange and unfair that Cassandra had followed her here to Italy, to disturb the peace that she was beginning to find in this unique place.

Later, as she started to walk along the main road, in the direction of the bridge, she heard a car driving closely behind her. She turned round and was shocked to see Cassandra behind the wheel. She stopped and the car drew up beside her and Cassandra leaned out of the window.

"There you are. Get in, Marina, let's talk!"

Marina reluctantly walked round to the passenger door of the hire car; she recognized the number plate from Pisa. Her sister must have picked it up at the airport when she arrived. She didn't want to get in the car as she knew from past experience that Cassandra's driving was erratic and how would she manage a left-hand drive? There was little choice, so she opened the door.

"All right, but I don't know why you're here. I came to Italy to get some space and make a new start. Please don't interfere with my life." She felt angry and frustrated with her sister for just turning up.

"I would have called, but you changed your mobile number. Mr Stokes was happy to give me your address, so I just jumped on the first plane out here. I've always wanted to visit Italy, so stop being selfish. It's a free country," she mocked.

Her tone made Marina feel angry, Cassandra would never change; she was the same self-centred, bitter girl that she knew so well. There was little she could do but humour her and hope that there was some way that she could be persuaded to return home to England.

By now, they were approaching the bridge and Cassandra pulled over into a dusty layby. There was one aspect to her that Marina knew might swing the balance. Cassandra had always been superstitions from an early age, especially after reading sinister stories and watching films of the occult at a friend's house. Their father had never approved of this obsession, but he was mostly ignorant of what his wayward daughter had access to, through other sources.

"This bridge has a strange atmosphere, what happened here?" she asked.

Marina told her the tale about the Devil's Bridge. She was concerned that this might alarm her and she did not want Cassandra to have an episode. As if to reflect the mood, grey clouds were gathering above the sisters and the sky was darkening. A storm was brewing and threatening heavy rain.

"This must be a warning sign, Cassandra, we must leave, there are bad spirits at work here."

"What are you talking about?" She had to raise her voice as the wind was picking up.

"The spirit of Lucifer, of course, it was here that he fell to his death. Can't you sense it… that deathly feeling…"

Even Marina felt uncomfortable, as she grabbed her sister's arm and tried to draw her away from the bridge. The peak of the stone structure stretched before them and appeared ghostly in the gloom. There was a piercing cry which startled them both but she was sure that it was the shriek of a bird. Cassandra suddenly looked petrified and her arm went limp.

"Come on, let's go back."

Cassandra had a lost look in her eyes and she allowed herself to be led to the car. The defiant tone of earlier had evaporated and she seemed meek and trusting.

Marina offered to drive, as she opened the passenger door for her sister. This was another of her mood swings, but at least it she was subdued rather than the manic.

"Where are you staying?"

"In Pisa, but can I stay with you tonight?"

"I will see if there is another room available, but I really think you should return home in the morning, Cassie. There's nothing for you here, I'm sorry."

"Perhaps you're right, but I want time to have a look around. I won't interfere with your plans."

Marina was not sure about that, but she decided not to voice her concerns and they returned to the *albergo* in silence, each immersed in their own thoughts.

As they arrived back, she could see Ruggiero waiting for her. He was sheltering in the entrance of a café. She called out and ran towards him and he looked over with a surprised expression. Her sister was close behind and had a strange, unkempt appearance.

Marina explained, "This is Cassandra, she turned up, unexpectedly." He could see that she was unhappy about this turn of events, but he was determined to be polite, although it felt awkward. She had described much of what happened in her childhood and how her sister's mental instability had affected the whole family. He could sympathise, as his family were also troubled by Giovanni's problems. However, Cassandra did seem very odd.

He greeted her with a forced smile and they all went into the small hotel. They discussed the plans for the evening and he spoke to Anna, the receptionist, and managed to book another room.

Cassandra immediately went up to the room with her case, as she felt exhausted after the day's events, and that left the couple to spend the evening together. It was a relief for them to have time to plan how to handle this unforeseen situation.

Ruggiero still felt insecure following Marina's rejection of his proposal. He tried to determine her feelings after the unwelcome reunion with her sister.

Her face looked blank, almost as if she was numb, distant, lost in thought. He put his arm around her shoulder and guided her down the street to a cosy bistro on the next corner.

"Come and sit down, you probably haven't eaten all day."

He chose two pasta dishes from the menu and a bottle of red wine. This should make her feel better, a good meal and some wine to lift her spirits. Ruggiero was curious to know what had happened between the sisters and what Marina planned to do, now that this volatile young woman had arrived. Perhaps she would destroy the sensitive ties of their relationship. It was such a crucial time for them both, with Marina's business plans and his own company.

As the food arrived, Marina was gradually restored to her more normal animated self. He was relieved to see her appetite was good, as he poured two large glasses of ruby coloured wine.

The young waiter had lit the candle on their table and it flickered as small shadows danced on the ochre walls in the small alcove where they sat.

"That's better isn't it."

"Yes," she said thankfully, and they started to discuss the day's events and how they would move forward. "It reminds me of that Dinah Washington song, do you know it, ironic but true," she laughed quietly.

He shook his head. "I don't know it. All I know is that whatever happens I want to have a future with you. After all, we have our own lives to lead and that does not have to directly involve our families. We must do what is best for us." He spoke with real passion and Marina felt that he was being totally genuine and speaking from the heart.

"I feel the same Ruggiero, I feel the same."

Chapter Twelve

Marina woke still feeling drained from the surprise encounter the day before. It took some effort to sit up and get her mind in order. She must spend time with her sister and find a solution to this mess. There was no place for Cassie in her new life; the decision to move here was brought about by the desire to break the suffocating bonds of responsibility from her previous life. A new beginning.

She decided that the only way to do this was to find security for Cassandra back in England. She had probably wasted much of the inheritance during those manic phases which she regularly experienced. Marina would need to find her some sort of sheltered accommodation; a place where she could receive support, but with a measure of independence.

Cassandra had always been fascinated by the secret world of monasteries and often stated that she would love to escape the stress of everyday life and immerse herself in a spiritual life.

Marina and her parents had never really believed this, thinking it was based on her fascination with a 1940s' film, *Black Narcissus*. This was a dark, psychological, romantic drama, about emotional tensions of jealousy and lust within a convent of nuns in the isolated mountains of the Himalayas.

Marina remembered looking up the name *Black Narcissus* and finding that it referred to the perfume, Narcisse Noir, made by Caron, and its effects on others; it also alluded to narcissism, one of the strong traits of a bipolar disorder.

Having researched this avenue before, she knew of a special community in Cornwall, not far from the cottage she had bought in Polperro soon after their parents' death. It was a Christian community based in a former Carmelite monastery, in a tranquil setting within close proximity to a village. The facilities were wonderful in this small hamlet, with opportunities for artwork and self-expression.

Cassandra had always been creative, so she was sure this would be ideal. It could provide the therapeutic lifestyle which would hopefully heal her sister's mental instability, in conjunction with regular counselling.

The best plan would be for them both to return to England together. That way, she could be sure that Cassandra would be safe and she could try out one of the trial retreats which the abbey offered. The main obstacle would be persuading her that this was the best path.

Marina dressed quickly and went to her sister's room. She knocked and waited, but there was no response. She then called out, but there was still no answer and she began to feel concerned.

Having enquired downstairs, Anna said that she had seen a young woman leaving earlier. She had not seen her face, as she had been wearing a silk headscarf.

She went outside; the hire car was still parked there from the previous day. If she was walking it must be easier to find her and after enquiring in a few of the local bars with no result, Marina then tried to put herself in the mind of her sister. Maybe she had returned to the Devil's Bridge, despite her fears and suspicions.

Marina rushed back to the *albergo* to collect her car; she needed to get there quickly as she was now beginning to feel anxious. Cassandra was capable of doing something really insane if she was off her medication.

Jumping into the car, she dialled Ruggiero's number and put the call on loudspeaker. The call went straight to message; he was probably on a morning run, which he did on his days off work. "Please phone me back, if you get this message… It's Cassie, I'm worried about her. She went out without me, so I'm driving to the Devil's Bridge."

Her driving was erratic through the town and some pedestrians looked angrily after her, but there was no time to waste. It was a short drive and she soon saw the distinctive five arches of the bridge showing around the bend in the road.

There was a figure standing on the middle one, sixty feet above the path, and she recognized it as Cassandra, leaning over, looking down into the eddying water beneath. She pushed down hard on the accelerator and drew up by the path to the bridge, tyres skidding on the uneven surface. Jumping out, she called to Cassandra. "Stop, stop! I'm here."

She looked down from the high arch; her eyes had a wild expression. Her hair was blowing around her face in a tangled Medusa-like way, that made Marina feel as if she was trapped in some nightmarish Greek tragedy. She appeared to be deaf to Marina's shouting and continued to climb onto the bridge wall until she was sitting on the edge. It was becoming increasingly dangerous, as she seemed to be in some kind of trance.

By now, there were more spectators, as other cars stopped by the bridge to watch the dramatic scene unfold. Ruggiero was one of them and he ran to Marina's side.

"Don't get too close, move slowly," he said reassuringly to Marina.

She was panicking now; her sister had done many erratic things, but this was the most extreme. Someone must have called the emergency services as she could hear sirens sounding in the valley.

"Please, Cassie, come down, we can help you. This is not the way, there's so much to live for." She had managed to move closer by edging up the steep path and her sister turned to look at her.

"There is nothing to live for…" she sobbed, shuffling towards the brink.

Ruggiero quietly skirted around Marina, unnoticed by her sister, who was looking down, once more, into the river. He put his finger to his lips, warning her to keep silent. It was a risky move but there seemed little alternative. It all happened in a split second, as he rushed forward and caught her around the shoulders and under one arm, as she started to slide off. The fabric of her top ripped but he managed to pull her to safety and she lay weeping on the cold stone pathway, looking lost and forlorn.

Marina scrambled to her side and put protective arms around the broken girl. She looked gratefully up at Ruggiero.

"Thank you, thank you for saving my sister…"

They were soon joined by the ambulance crew, who carried Cassandra gently to a waiting vehicle. The others followed, and after a brief discussion with Ruggiero, Marina climbed into the ambulance with her sister who was lying on a stretcher inside.

Now the excitement was over, the crowd of onlookers began to disperse, muttering to each other and gesticulating towards the bridge. Some signed the cross in front of themselves and inclined their heads to an alcove where a statue of Mary Magdalene had once stood. It had been moved to the parish church of Borgo a Mozzano. The satanic name had prevailed long ago, eclipsing the previous one of Ponte della Maddalena.

Ruggiero offered to follow them to the nearest hospital, so that he could help with any issues that might arise. He was not sure how the whole incident would be handled and he was reluctant to contact his parents and involve them. He was sure they would be sympathetic, but it was sad that this terrible crisis had happened just as Marina was being accepted by his friends and family.

He had mixed feelings about Cassandra. Compassion was one, as he understood that she was mentally unstable, but he couldn't understand why she was not taking her medication, and anger at the disruption she was causing. Marina's life had been blighted enough by this oppressive shadow on her life. Ruggiero decided that this was the final straw. He would support any decision that was made about persuading Cassandra to return to England and seeking the professional help which she so desperately needed.

This would probably mean that they would be apart for a few weeks while she set up the arrangements. She could use this opportunity to stay at her cottage in Cornwall, which was being rented by an old family friend.

Marina sat nervously by Cassandra holding her hand, as the medics carried out their examination. She looked pale and almost ghostly lying there and extremely vulnerable. Marina didn't even attempt to understand what they were saying, as they discussed the patient in rapid Italian. She just allowed herself to discharge any responsibility, which in many ways was a welcome relief.

Once she had been settled in a private room at the hospital, the doctors advised that Cassandra should stay to for a least a couple of days for observation. She would need to be assessed for medication and Marina offered to contact her doctor in England for advice, as her sister had been sedated.

Ruggiero had been a great asset communicating with the staff and was able to reassure Marina that she was in safe hands.

He had arranged for her car to be returned to the hotel and he drove her back in his. She was completely exhausted and went straight to her room to lie down. It had been a tiring and emotional day.

Chapter Thirteen

There were plans to be made, so Marina woke early and made some notes in a pad she always kept on the bedside table. She found that this was the best way to clear her mind and concentrate the myriad of thoughts that clouded her head. She numbered them in order of importance.

1.Visit Cassie in hospital and discuss her medication and discharge with the doctor & psychiatrist

2.Contact the Christian community in Cornwall and see if they can accommodate Cassie

3.Speak to my friend in Polperro to say I will be coming to stay for a few weeks

4. Discuss all this with Ruggiero and ask him to speak on my behalf with the mediatore regarding the villa and structural surveys. Make a final offer following the results of the report.

That was enough for now, apart from booking the flights home and packing her belongings.

Dawn was beginning to break, so she looked out at the rosy glow of a new day. The square below was mostly deserted apart from the local baker who appeared on his bike, ready for a busy morning ahead, and a few stray cats on the look-out for scraps. Their skinny feline forms slipped like ghosts between the buildings, leaping onto walls and staring, with hungry eyes, from their lofty posts.

These cats reminded her of those early days at home in Cornwall. However, the ones of her childhood had been well-fed and spoilt tabbies, lounging in front of the glowing Aga, a wood-burning stove that emanated cosy warmth on those cold winter evenings. What was that word the Danish used… *hygge*: cosy, comfortable, conviviality; a feeling of contentment. Those purring cats were the polar opposite of their distant cousins in the shadows below.

She was many moons from finding this security and the street cats below reflected her mindset more accurately: dodging through a minefield of obstacles to find some stability and hope in what could be a cruel and difficult existence. The loss of their parents had shaken the foundations of both the girls' lives and Marina felt duty bound to find a safe haven for her defenceless sister.

The rumbling of her belly brought these musings to a close. She had missed a proper dinner the night before, after falling into bed in a daze. She would go in search of some breakfast as soon as the *panetteria* was open, but first she felt like a long soak in the bath with the windows open, so she could hear the birds stirring in the surrounding trees and listen to the reassuring sound of the town gradually coming to life.

Ruggiero had woken later than usual, as he had been drained from the dramatic episode the previous day. He hurriedly showered and dressed and decided to grab some coffee and breakfast on the way. He knew that Marina would be anxious and need the support he could offer, as it would be difficult to negotiate the medical issues at the hospital and she was also on foreign soil.

He sent a text to say he was on his way and would collect her. There was no response, so he assumed she was already at the hospital, as the signal was not always good there.

When he arrived and made his way to the private room, he could hear the warm tones of Marina's distinctive voice. She was trying to speak with one of the doctors and looked over gratefully when she saw Ruggiero coming to her aid.

It had been established that this psychotic episode on the bridge may have been triggered by a number of factors, such as fatigue and medicinal withdrawal. The doctor had done a number of tests and following the result of the blood test had diagnosed an antipsychotic to stabilise her mental state. He had also been concerned by the result of a CT scan which revealed a possible abnormality in her brain. The specialist advised that a full MRI scan would be advisable soon.

He believed it was imperative to get the patient home and to a familiar environment, but she would need to recuperate for a few days before facing another plane journey.

After spending some time sitting at her sister's side, Marina was in need of a break, so Ruggiero persuaded her to leave the hospital for lunch. The strain was beginning to take its toll on her and the haunted expression of the previous evening had returned.

She found it difficult to feel positive despite the support she was receiving, as the next few weeks loomed ahead, especially with the worry of her sister possibly having a tumour. The journey home would be a challenge and the ghosts of her past life were waiting in the shadows.

During lunch at a bistro in town Ruggiero tried to be upbeat.

"Don't worry, Marina, your sister will come through this episode. It was a mistake for her to follow you here and in some way this crisis needed to come to a head, so that she can come to terms with her condition."

Marina still looked despondent, so he held her soft hands in his and continued.

"You have done all you can and you are a caring sister. Once everything has been arranged and she has further treatment, you can breathe again and realise your aspirations. I will be waiting for your return."

The next few days seemed to flash past with preparations for the journey and visits to her sister, who was making a good recovery. Cassandra was still in a confused state, but she had responded well to treatment and would be able to travel in a week. She seemed relieved to have all the decisions made for her and accepted the proposal of returning to Cornwall.

Marina was also in a more positive frame of mind and actually looking forward to the trip. Despite many of the sad memories, the thought of windswept walks by the beautiful Cornish coastline and cosy evenings in the local pub with friends, filled her with optimism.

Autumn was just around the corner, which was a special time of year for Marina. She would be in England for her birthday and it always reminded her of the last gift she received from her parents. They knew that she had a passion for the poetry of the English romantics, in particular, John Keats, so her father had managed to locate a first edition of his complete poems, dated 1902. It was a beautiful book bound by Morrell in a classic Scottish wheel design of green crushed Moroccan leather, lavishly gilded on both spine and covers.

She kept this book with her wherever she travelled and it was a constant source of pleasure. Keats' life had been cruelly cut short, with his tragic death in Rome from tuberculosis aged only twenty-five. However, during his life he had managed to capture the essence of life, nature and humanity. Many evenings she had sat with her mother and enjoyed reading the poetry aloud, particularly the ode, *To Autumn*. She had memorised the words and recalled the opening lines;

Season of mists and mellow fruitfulness
Close bosom-friend of the maturing sun
Conspiring with him how to load and bless
With fruit the vines that round the thatch-eaves
run…

Marina, herself, was what she called a closet poet. She had won a competition for one of her poems when she was just sixteen.

At the time, she had been embarrassed by all the attention she had received, reading it in public at the society's monthly meeting and the poem being published in the local press. She was afraid of becoming a victim of her peers at school, especially as she was a joint winner with a local boy who was regarded as a nerd.

Ever since that experience, her writing had been a secret passion. Her poems' titles ranged from nature, fauna and flora, to venting her emotions with the frustration of her sister's extreme behaviour. In many ways it became a sort of therapy, a secret world which she created.

Sometimes, in the holidays, she would pack a few apples in a bag with her writing materials and disappear for the day. She had a favourite tree to climb, where she had fashioned a makeshift tree-house. This place provided the inspiration for many of her pieces by the study of the birds and animals which strayed into view of her lofty eyrie.

Marina decided to resume her writing, while waiting for her sister's recovery. Ruggiero was busy with work and she was still waiting for the surveyor's report, so there was little she could do with the Villa Lucifer project.

She looked out her old manuscripts, which were kept in a folder made from exquisite Venetian paper. Many of the poems dated from her early life and she mused over their words. Her love of nature spilled out from every page and then she found one that transported her to a summer's day spent with a close friend. He had been the first boy that she had really had feelings for. That day was particularly windy and he had called round to see if she wanted to fly a kite with him.

She remembered how excited she had been and they had laughed together, running so fast up the hill that they became breathless. This experience had been immortalised in her poem:

The Kite

Bright cobalt-blue, straining on its bridle
A wild-winged bird, fighting for survival
Spars straining, tugging the fluttering cloth
Flying-line pulling tight, mesmerising moth

Nose-diving, swirling, dervish-like dance
We struggled, gripping tight taut string, in a trance

Gusty broken winds, dipping and diving
Spine-breaking, curling, ripping and writhing

At last, skywards strong winds lift the dancing kite
Soaring high above, joining birds in flight
Leaving exhausted watchers to admire in duty
No longer earthbound, but a free object of beauty

Chapter Fourteen

The first few days spent in Cornwall made her realise what she had missed about her homeland. There was beauty everywhere: the rugged coastline with cliff views across sparkling seascapes and the rusty reddish-brown bracken covering the rolling moorlands.

She particularly enjoyed woodland walks, just as the glowing sun was sinking below the horizon. The flaming foliage contrasted starkly against the dark brown trunks of the ghostly trees. Dry leaves rattled above, like weathered bones hanging from a gibbet's noose and a rich earthy aroma emanated from the forest litter which rustled beneath her feet.

One evening she saw a little owl perched on the overhanging branch of a beech tree. It had mottled brown plumage and glowing yellow eyes. Marina gasped in pleasure and felt privileged to witness this wonderful bird. She had been very interested in Greek mythology as a young girl and remembered the story of Athena. A little owl (Athene noctua) traditionally represented or accompanied Athena, the goddess of wisdom.

The German idealist philosopher, Hegel, famously noted that, 'the owl of Minerva spreads its wings only with the falling of the dusk', which she interpreted as philosophy, coming to understand a historical condition just as it passes away.

Unfortunately, there was little time to enjoy these pleasures, as her main focus was to finalise arrangements before her departure.

Cassandra was very subdued, but her happiness in returning home was undeniable. She liked sitting outside during the afternoon with a rug over her knees, reading or dozing in the tranquil cottage garden. The rumble of the sea could be heard, as waves crashed onto the shore in the distance and gulls skimmed overhead, flying along the coast.

She had untaken an MRI scan and there was a suspected brain tumour. The treatment would involve radiotherapy and possibly chemotherapy. The pressure caused by this may have aggravated her mental condition. The doctors advised rest and regular appointments, so Marina assigned a private nurse to care for her sister while she was away.

Once the final plans had been made for Cassandra's new accommodation, they had an excursion to the Lost Gardens of Heligan near Mevagissey. It was an enchanting place to spend their last day together, following the winding paths through the tranquil woodlands of the historical gardens into some mysterious clearings. They discovered a large reclining figure of Gaia, the primordial goddess representing Mother Earth in sleeping pose, made from earth, moss and grasses. The autumnal colours were stunning, in particular, the bright purple berries of the Callicarpa shrub in the enchanted gardens.

That last evening, she walked alone once more in the woods near the cottage. The sharp spine-chilling bark of a solitary fox echoed in the night chill. She wondered if this was a harbinger of good or evil and then quickly expelled this superstitious thought. Smiling to herself, she wondered if she had been reading too many mythical tales, in some of the old tattered books that lined the shelves in her room.

Marina had enjoyed this fleeting visit, but she was now ready to return to Italy and continue her new life there. The parting with her sister was difficult, but she knew that Cassandra would be in safe hands and hopefully find some contentment with the supportive network of the close community.

She would return to England again soon to see how her sister's treatment was progressing.

The flight was booked to arrive in Pisa the next evening. Ruggiero was waiting patiently for her at the airport. She ran towards him and, as they embraced, she felt all the stress from the past few weeks evaporate. On the journey home, he updated her on all the news and explained that the structural survey had been completed on the villa and she could now make a final decision. There was a great deal of work to be done but the foundations were mostly sound, so it could be completed in a month or so.

She was so relieved and believed it would be possible to open her new premises by Christmas. She wanted to have a grand opening, with live music and a menu of locally sourced food.

"My parents have offered for you to stay in the apartment above the stables at their villa, until the work is finished on your new place. What do you think?"

"That is really kind, but are you sure that would work?" she looked concerned.

"Don't worry, Marina, I am not going to put you under any pressure, or propose to you again for a while," he teased. "I just want you to have a secure base to work from and to provide support, if you will allow me."

"Then, I would love to. Thanks." She leant over and kissed him warmly.

Cornwall would always be a special place for her, but Toscane had laid a spell on her in every possible way.

Chapter Fifteen

The next few weeks passed quickly and there was a hive of activity at the villa on the mountainside. Ruggiero was able to assist in suggesting an architect and building contractor. She was aware that work operations performed differently in Italy, so she had to be patient. Marina felt some anxiety in finishing the building project on schedule, as she had already booked the services of kitchen and serving staff plus musicians, for her grand opening.

She had been in touch with Connor, her Irish musician friend, who would provide the entertainment for the first night and stay on for the following week. No mention was made that he was an ex-boyfriend, as she was concerned that Ruggiero may become jealous. It had taken some time to persuade Connor and his band to come to Italy, as they had not left Ireland for any engagements before. Marina organised all the travel and accommodation arrangements, as she was determined to book a band which performed music she enjoyed and she was secretly looking forward to seeing Connor again. She still felt guilty for leaving him so suddenly all those many months ago. It seemed like a lifetime had passed, with all the events that had happened since.

Her vision was to create a diverse fusion of Italian cuisine, Irish music and her own creative individuality. The villa was springing into life, like the recumbent sculpture of a sleeping Canova lion stirring from its slumbers. She had marvelled at these magnificent sculptures on a visit to Rome, and discovered that they were created by the eighteenth century artist, Antonio Canova, for the monumental tomb of Pope Clement XIII in St. Peter's Basilica.

Marina felt the weight of responsibility for making this renovation of the old villa a success. It could become a focal point of interest for visitors to the region and a cultural hub in the local community. Her plan was to make a versatile place for entertainment, great food and an exhibition or performing space for artisans and musicians. She had also decided to change the original name to one less controversial, *l'Angelo*, the Angel.

It seemed like the whole community was coming together to reach the Christmas deadline. Fortunately, the weather had been fairly dry and there were only minor delays with the building works. Despite the cold weather, there was little chance of snowfall. She took great pleasure from marvelling at the crystalline panoramic views from the attic rooms of the villa. As she walked with Ruggiero below, they shared the pleasure of seeing the once vacant windows glimmering with light, as dusk fell.

Colourful blue shutters had been fastened to the outside walls and the freshly-painted stucco looked crisp in the morning light. She had risen early to spend some time alone. It was a chance to think and plan for the grand opening in a few weeks.

When the original structural survey had been completed there was some disturbing information that came to light. There had been seismic activity in that area of Tuscany during the past decade. The surveyor had stated that there was a very small chance that their location would be affected, but he had put it down as an advisory. Fortunately, due to her inheritance, Marina did not have to take out a mortgage to purchase the property or undertake the reconstruction, but it was getting close to the limit of her budget. It would also be difficult to obtain the building insurance to cover an 'act of god' if any damage arose from a natural disaster, such as an earthquake.

Marina looked up the definition for an 'act of god': 'an instance of uncontrollable natural forces in operation'. She then did some research on seismic activity in Italy and discovered that there had been a number of tremors and earthquakes in central Italy and parts of Tuscany. The worst had been near L'Aquila, when nearly three hundred people had died due to a massive shock in the mountain belt of the Apennines.

Ruggiero assured her that the villa should not be at risk, but she spent some sleepless nights worrying that she was chancing her precious inheritance with this project.

Despite all these issues, the bookings were rolling in, as excitement grew in the area for the opening of a new restaurant. She was aware that the period from the feast of Santo Stefano on December 26th until Epifania on the 6th January was a hugely popular period for Italian tourists, so the atmosphere was cranking up to the point that even her small rural restaurant would require reservations. All the towns and villages were being lavishly decorated for Christmas, so it was a perfect time to open.

The contacts she had made over the summer had helped with advertising by word of mouth and of course she had the Giannini family support. Even Giovanni, Ruggiero's errant twin brother, seemed to be on board and he made the positive suggestion of running a competition, to attract more visitors. The Torneo Gioco del Panforte (Panforte Tournament Games) took place annually in the town of Pienza, near Siena from December 26th to 30th, in the Piazza Pio II Loggiato del Comune. He told Marina that competing teams throw a panforte cake to a table from fifteen feet away. The team throwing and sliding the panforte closest to the edge of the table is the winner. He described the panforte as a sort of flat, disc shaped Italian fruitcake made during the Christmas season. The Villa L'Angelo's adoption of this game could start a new tradition in their own area of Tuscany.

Ruggiero was dubious of his brother's suggestion, but she put this down to filial jealousy.

It was now imperative that everything came together by mid-December, otherwise she would be under huge pressure. With one last push, the Villa L'Angelo was finally taking shape. The sign she had commissioned from a local craftsman depicting the light-bringing Morning Star, was completed and ready to be installed on the facade. This represented Lucifer, the angel of music, before his fall from grace.

Marina hoped that this would dispel the ancient stories emanating from the Devil's Bridge of Borgo del Mozzano, in the valley below.

Chapter Sixteen

Marina was relieved to hear, from her friends in England, that the treatment her sister was receiving appeared to be successful and Cassandra had settled into her new life. Any more stress during these last few weeks could potentially tip her over the edge. Ruggiero had taken some time off his own work and his positive attitude and dry humour kept her grounded. He was also supplying some of the specialist olive oils and fermented vegetables, *giandiniera*, from the Giannini label. This typical Italian *giardiniera* comprised of bell peppers, celery, carrots, cauliflower and gherkins, which was colourful and delicious.

    He also decided to surprise her with an unexpected gift. Ruggiero knew that she was very fond of all animals, but especially dogs. An old shepherd who lived in Tereglio had been taken ill and could no longer look after his loyal companion, so his mountain dog needed to be rehomed. A watchdog would be good company for Marina in such a remote place. The Maremmano Sheepdog, a large powerful breed with snowy white coat has a protective nature and possesses a deep resonant bark. She was completely overcome when Luna, this beautiful dog, was brought in and there was an instant connection between them.

Marina was now staying in an apartment within the Villa l'Angelo, in part of the renovated first floor, so she placed the dog's bed beside her own. During the night she felt the large dog move onto the end of her bed and lie beside her feet, like the guardian on a medieval tomb.

She remembered the story she had been told about the devil's bridge and that a Maremmano was used to trick the devil by the architect. This ghostly dog was supposed to still haunt the bridge. The mythical tale seemed a world apart from her affectionate Luna.

He followed her everywhere and was sometimes over protective, particularly with strangers, but had been well-trained and responded to her gestures and some of the Italian voice commands she had learnt.

The dog was a good distraction and she felt much more relaxed. The villa was looking wonderful and any problems they encountered were quickly resolved.

It was only two weeks now until the opening night, so she started discussing the menus with her chef. Giovanni had offered to oversee the bar and wine delivery, against his brother's wishes, but Marina wanted this to be a family affair to bring everyone together. Their mother, Sophia, had been away visiting friends in the south, but as soon as she returned had offered to assist. She sourced a piano for the salon room and performed some Chopin *Preludes* in the evening for Marina, as she relaxed with Ruggiero over a bottle of red Tuscan wine and some *antipasti* from the new kitchen.

The musicians were expected the next day and Marina was feeling excited but a little apprehensive. However, all her worries were dispelled when Connor and his friends arrived at the Villa. She ran forward to greet them and all the original camaraderie was restored. Connor was genuinely pleased to see her again and kept exclaiming about the place.

"Isn't this grand, such a great setting. You look so well, Marina."

She showed him around and the room where the band would set up.

"It's so wonderful to have you here. I hope the journey was okay. This is where I would like the band to be for the opening night." She indicated a small stage at the end of the main hall.

He looked impressed. "That will work fine, can we rehearse tomorrow?"

"Yes, of course. I thought that we would all have a meal here tonight and then I can get Giovanni to take you to your lodgings in the town."

Her dog, Luna, came to meet the newcomers and they made a fuss of him. He sat obediently by Marina's side and surveyed the men in his role as watchdog.

They all sat down to dinner and spent the evening catching up on the latest news and enjoying a few drinks. Marina looked over at Connor and was once again entranced by his charm and easy-going nature. It was obvious that the attraction was still there, but she was disturbed from these thoughts when Ruggiero suddenly entered the room.

"Ah, I see I am a little late for the celebration. So this is the famous Connor and his band." He strode over as Connor stood up and they shook hands, assessing each other at the same time. Ruggiero was taller and more distinguished but Connor had a strong physique and warm open smile. Marina felt uncomfortable but tried to appear relaxed about the situation.

"Actually, they're just about to leave and get some rest. Giovanni has offered to take them." She got up and went to fetch his brother who had been sorting out the bar. "They are ready to go now, Gio, thanks."

He pretended to make a small bow. "Your wish is my command, signorina."

She grinned at him, "Enough messing around, signore autista!" They unloaded some of the equipment and then piled into the van which she had borrowed to transport them. As they disappeared down the mountain, Marina went over to Ruggiero and embraced him warmly. "I think everything is beginning to come together." He nodded but he still felt unnerved, as he had observed the natural empathy between these old friends. Perhaps he would need to protect his interests more vigilantly.

Chapter Seventeen

Marina was very busy for the next week but the band came to the villa daily to rehearse and so she had chance to spend time with them. It was so good to be with the old crowd again, from her time in Ireland. Those had been very happy, carefree days, without the responsibility she now felt with her new venture.

The opening night was drawing close and tension was beginning to build, even her dog seemed more unsettled. She put this down to him missing his previous owner, but Luna's behaviour was different and he appeared restless, when he had been fine before.

Ruggiero had been away for a few days, as his father was ill with suspected pneumonia, but he called every day to check everything was ready.

The whole area was in festive mode as Christmas Day approached and the celebrations began. There had been a change in the weather and it had become very cold and windy. Some of the decorations and lights had to be secured more carefully, as blasts of icy air swept down from the mountains. Marina watched as some of her staff braved the elements to fasten the external fairy lights more tightly to the stonework. Some were woven around the intricate black wrought iron balustrades that formed some of the Juliet balconies on the facade of the building. It was difficult work, but she was relieved that there were no mishaps during these precautions.

The stunning main staircase inside the villa was also decorated with lights. She now realised why the name balustrade was coined in seventeenth century Italy. It was a descriptive term for the bulbous feature's resemblance to blossoming pomegranate flowers or *balaustra* in Italian.

She had decided to include displays of dried fruit, fir garlands and cinnamon sticks, which reminded her of a Cornish childhood. Her mother had loved everything to do with this season and was always out gathering holly to decorate their cottage and brewing mulled wine laced with cinnamon to serve to guests. The aroma would fill their home and she was at once transported back to those halcyon days of innocence.

The last two days passed swiftly and the opening night was suddenly a reality. Marina was feeling stressed, as the brothers had fallen out over some missing wine crates and Ruggiero suspected that Giovanni was being dishonest. Some valuable wines had been ordered and two crates had disappeared from the wine cave. He believed that Gio's addiction to gambling had led him to sell on some of the stock, so he had told Marina she must sack him.

She was angry that Giovanni had betrayed her trust, as she had hoped this venture would bring them all together. Marina had no choice and told him to leave at once. This seemed like a bad omen on this special day and once more, she felt apprehensive.

She tried to expel any negative feelings and called a meeting in the hall for all her staff. They gathered in a group, chatting excitedly and admiring the fruits of their combined labour. The crystal chandeliers glistened and the lights shimmered as the dusk drew a black cloak over the mountains and the valley below.

Marina stood on the stage looking at the smiling faces. "I first want to say, thank you, for all the hard work and support you have given me over the past few weeks. This has been a dream come true for me and I hope that this evening will be a huge success. Remember to keep all our guests happy and their glasses full. The doors will open in one hour. Thank you again and back to work!"

As they all dispersed, Connor came over and put his arms around her shoulder in an affectionate and almost protective way. "You've done wonders here, Marina. I'm sure that your parents would be proud of you."

"That's kind of you," she said gratefully. "I'm so happy that you could be a part of this special evening." She then saw Ruggiero approaching with a dark expression on his face. Not only had he just been dealing with seeing his brother off but now he was greeted with this intimate moment. Marina shrugged it off, but she was aware of the growing antagonism between the two men.

Connor went to join the rest of the band, while Marina disappeared upstairs to change. She was not in the mood to have a discussion with Ruggiero and she realised that this possessive side of him was actually really unattractive.

Luna followed her and she was comforted by his calm presence. He lay beside her dressing table while she put on the sleek black dress bought for the occasion. Sitting down in front of the antique mirror, she arranged her long hair into a neat chignon with some stray strands framing her face. There were dark shadows under her eyes from a few sleepless nights of worry, but she soon covered these with a layer of discreet makeup.

There was a knock on the door and she looked round as Ruggiero walked in. "Sorry to disturb you, but I just wanted to apologise for my behaviour earlier. You know my feelings…" His voice trailed off and he looked contrite.

"Don't worry, Ruggiero, I understand. We have all been under a great deal of strain, especially with your father's illness and now your brother letting us down. After all the belief we had in him that he had changed. He just has that additive kind of personality." Tears of frustration filled her eyes but she was determined not to cry and held herself back. She stood up and they embraced gently.

He then pulled away and looked admiringly at her outfit. "You look wonderful, Marina"

Chapter Eighteen

The scene was now set for a brilliant evening. Marina could see the renovated mansion was full of living energy, almost like a creature stirring from a long hibernation, shaking off the shackles of atrophy to live once more.

As the scene was set and the guests began to arrive, Marina circulated the hall, greeting each person. Drinks were served and the noise of animated conversation gradually rose in volume as more revellers arrived. The atmosphere was warm and inviting, as the rooms glowed with myriad lights and the swathes of stunning decorations.

Ruggiero came forward and touched Marina on the shoulder as she was talking to a young Italian couple. She turned round to smile at him, forgetting any of the earlier tension.

"*Buonanotte*, Marina, you look wonderful."

"Thank you, I can't believe this is all really happening." She excused herself from the guests and moved to one side. "I'm so grateful for your support, I don't think I could have achieved this without you."

"You can achieve anything, Marina, with your incredible vision and energy. I know it will be a success." He held her hand tightly and then they rejoined the others

The band had started playing in the adjoining room and everyone began to move through to listen.

Suddenly her dog, Luna, appeared in the doorway; he was acting strangely, whining and threading his way rapidly through the guests towards her. They all looked on with surprise, at this large dog whose imposing presence was disturbing the party. However, Marina realised at once that there was something wrong, he was normally so well behaved and this was completely out of character. He then started barking loudly and pawing at her dress; he was clearly agitated and scared.

Just as she was about to take action, there was a terrible rumbling sound and she could feel a violent tremor beneath her feet. The wooden floor shuddered as the walls quivered and she realised that it was an earthquake. The windows rattled and glass shattered, spraying across the room like sharp stalactites. Some pieces struck those people who had not managed to take cover. After the initial paralysing shock, everyone began to panic and head for the doors, shouting and screaming. Ruggiero tried to calm them down as he attempted to prevent a stampede. Many of them could be crushed and trampled on.

"Take cover under the tables," he shouted loudly above the noise of chairs falling, broken glass and clamouring voices. The trembling stopped for a moment and then there was another ocean wave of movement which was stronger than before. He reached out and grabbed Marina's arm as she fell to the floor, gasping with shock. There was one more ripple of movement and then it finally stopped with a last shudder. There was a sound of whimpering from those who had been injured, but at last it seemed to be over.

Marina's arm felt bruised where she had fallen to the ground and then she realised that there was blood oozing from a large gash on her leg. She felt confused, bewildered and light-headed.

That must have been why Luna had been behaving so wildly, she realised; dogs had a second sense about these... and then she cried out desperately,

"Where is Luna?"

Ruggiero had been kneeling beside her, trying to staunch the wound on her leg, but now shook his arm vigorously. "Please, find him."

"Wait, I need to stop this bleeding." He had grabbed one of the linen napkins that had fallen off the table and was applying pressure to the wound.

"Press down on this hard and I will have a look around."

Everything was in chaos and the screaming had been replaced by moaning, weeping and calls for help. There was a coating of thick dust everywhere so he couldn't see much in the semi-darkness, as the power had cut out. He still had his mobile phone and he took it out of his pocket and pressed the torch setting. As he scrambled towards where he had last seen the dog, he could see a white ghostly shape lying underneath an overturned table. He managed to reach Luna and was sickened to see that his body was lifeless and felt limp to the touch. He leant over the loyal dog and stroked his silky coat. They had not heeded the dog's warning, but the unimaginable had happened. How was he going to tell Marina, she would be heart-broken and now everything was ruined. Her dreams were lying in tatters and debris around them. He was unsure of what to do next; someone had to take control and he had been fortunate to avoid injury. So many people needed help and he was sure the rescue services would be overwhelmed in the area by such a severe earthquake. His mobile was running low on battery but he made a call to the emergency line which was engaged.

As he made his way carefully through the rubble, trying to assess the damage as he passed the tables where many people were still huddled, he found Marina lying in the same place. She was unconscious and he suddenly realised that she could be in some danger with the loss of blood.

He checked the wound which looked quite serious and he applied some more pressure, calling out to a man who appeared out of the gloom. He recognised him as one of Marina's new staff. "Please can you help me, I think she is badly injured and needs medical attention." He stumbled towards Ruggiero and together they lifted Marina and took her over to a chaise longue. By now some candles were being lit as the electricity was still out, but the light was dim in the dust-filled room.

"Is there a doctor here?" he called out. There was no response at first and then he heard a chain of voices repeating his plea and a doctor was found amongst the guests.

Sirens could be heard in the valley below as the emergency services responded to the unexpected disaster. It would be impossible for them to reach this location, as the mountain road would be impassable with all the rock fall. The whirring of a helicopter could be heard above the building, so they hoped that help was on its way.

Chapter Nineteen

Marina woke in a hospital room; the lights were bright and harsh to her sore eyes. She wasn't sure how long she had been there but, looking over, she saw Ruggiero. He looked exhausted, slumped on an armchair, creases of worry lines on his brow. As she tried to raise her body, he woke and quickly moved to her side.

"You're awake at last. Let me help you." He rearranged the pillows to make her comfortable as she sat up. She felt dizzy and sick.

"How long have I been here? I can't remember much of what happened."

"It's been about three days, I think. To be honest, I have lost track of time, everything seems so surreal."

"Were many people hurt and what has happened to the villa?"

"Look Marina, the doctor said you must keep calm and not get upset, otherwise it could harm your recovery." He looked really concerned and she was touched by this, but wanted to know everything.

Ruggiero tried to tone down the number of people who had been injured that fateful night and the ruinous state of the villa. She would need to know the full extent of the damage soon, but this was not the time. She looked so vulnerable in the metal bed of this sparse hospital room. He knew she would be devastated by the aftermath of the earthquake and particularly how it had affected all her new friends. He gave her an abridged version of the destruction and tried to look optimistic and encouraging. He thought she would probably see right through this ploy, but she was soon tired and lost focus. Then a nurse came in and said it was time for her to rest, so he reluctantly left her room as she smiled wanly at his receding figure.

Her recovery took much longer than had been anticipated, as the mental distress heightened the physical injuries which she had received at the scene. In addition to this it was discovered, during various tests, that she was expecting a child, which was a complete shock. Fortunately, it was early in the pregnancy and all appeared stable, but it was so much for Marina to take in.

As soon as she felt well enough to discuss the future, she spoke to Ruggiero about the baby. Despite her initial fears he was overjoyed and cried with emotion. True, it wasn't planned, but he wanted to spend his life with Marina and he hoped that she felt the same.

Her recovery was slow and painful. His parents invited Marina to recuperate at the family estate, so she moved back into the apartment she had been using there before the villa was complete. They were kind and supportive, endeavouring to offset the despair she felt at losing everything. Without proper insurance there was no recompense for the losses she had incurred.

She was excited about the child but she was suffering from severe sickness, coupled with the sore wound that was taking some time to heal.

It was too cold to sit outside for long in January, but Marina enjoyed the fresh air blowing from the mountains. She was wrapped in a warm blanket watching some of the wildlife in the garden, when Ruggiero arrived back one sunlit, cloudless afternoon. Red squirrels had been chasing each other though the spreading branches of trees in the garden and the occasional bird rustled in the undergrowth.

He came forward and gently touched her shoulder.

"How are you feeling? It's so peaceful here, isn't it."

She turned round a little to greet him. "Yes, it is beautiful here and I'm feeling much better. It has been good to have this time for reflection. I've been thinking about everything and I believe I need some time back in England."

He was surprised to hear this, as she had not mentioned the subject before. Ruggiero moved around to face her, drawing up one of the garden chairs. He sat down, searching her face, trying to discern the thought patterns etched in her eyes. He could now see that she had been crying, as there were light traces of moisture laced on her cheeks like gossamer threads. He took a handkerchief from a pocket and offered it to her. She took it gratefully, trying to appear happy with a whisper of a smile.

"I really appreciate everything you have done for me. I just need some time away to absorb what's happened. I feel that I've lost control of my life and my mind is clouded with indecision. I hope that you can understand." She pressed his hand lightly and then looked away, unable to stand the sense of betrayal that her words might evoke.

"I don't understand Marina, I thought that you would be happy here. What will happen about our future together and our son or daughter? "

"I can't say yet, I just need to put everything into perspective and the only way I can do this, is to spend time away from this place." Despite the high-running emotions, her voice was firm. "I believe it is for the best, for now."

He now raised his voice in anguish. "The best for whom? You, me, my family..." his voice trailed off. He knew she was still in a fragile state, but she could be so frustrating and enigmatic. Maybe it was a good idea for them to have some time apart, but he was reluctant to accept this. "Do what you have to, Marina, but think of what we have between us and the life we can build together." He stood up abruptly as he didn't want the situation to escalate into an argument and turned to leave. She was obviously upset but he saw the determined look on her face, which he had often observed when she had made decisions in the past.

"Think about it, Marina," was his parting shot, as he headed towards his car parked on the gravel drive. Small pebbles were thrown into the air from the wheels, as he sped down the avenue.

Chapter Twenty

Arrangements were made over the following weeks to sort out the aftermath of the earthquake. The mountain road had long been cleared and the building secured. Ruggiero agreed to oversee the works, so that Marina could return to England. Connor and his friends had left some time ago, while she had been recovering in hospital. She had been too confused to know what was happening at that time, but she hoped to reconnect with him soon. She packed some of her belongings, which Ruggiero had managed to rescue from the debris, into a couple of suitcases. The majority of her possessions could not be recovered. They drove in silence to the airport in Pisa, neither one of them knowing what to say. He was hurt that she seemed to be running away and she was perplexed that he could not understand her reasons for needing space. It had been a traumatic event in her life and she felt that she was once again reliving the loss of earlier years. Marina did not want a long, painful parting, so she asked him to drop her off outside the entrance. He collected a trolley for her bags, then they parted awkwardly without expressing their true feelings.

Although she was sorry to leave him, she suddenly experienced a feeling of relief, as the plane soared into the air and Tuscany disappeared from view below the shimmering clouds.

Chapter Twenty-One

Returning to Cornwall brought some relief to Marina as she tried to dispel the painful memories of the past month. Many of those recollections were hazy and she knew there would come a time when they would have to be faced, but she wasn't ready yet.

The friends living in her cottage had moved out, so she had the peace and tranquillity that was vital to her recovery. Walking on the cliff path, overlooking the eternal movement of the restless sea below, was a tonic to her troubled mind. However, she could not dispel the faces which drifted into her conscience without invitation. Ruggiero's concern etched in his eyes, the attentive nurse who had treated her at the hospital and dear faithful Luna, who would no longer share her life.

As the days passed, she could feel the baby growing inside; although still early in her pregnancy, there was a tightening sensation within. She knew she should feel happy, but there was just a dull sensation of emptiness. The therapist she had consulted had said it would pass in time, so she tried to sweep away the feelings of guilt.

A few weeks later, Marina felt strong enough to visit her sister, who was convalescing at a local hospice. She had undergone further treatment following a resurgence of her illness and was still in a critical state. It had been many months since their last meeting and Cassandra had changed drastically. She was a shadow of her former self and there was a constant vacant expression in her eyes.

"How are you feeling, Cassie?" she enquired gently, holding her sister's pale hand.

"I don't know, where am I and who are these people?" She indicated, looking out into the corridor through the open door.

"You're in a safe place and they are caring for you."

Despite their differences over the years, tears began to swell in her eyes as she quietly mourned for the loss of her sister's previous vitality. She knew the prognosis was not good for her and she suddenly felt scared and alone. Returning to the cottage, she saw an unfamiliar vehicle parked outside in the lane. As she stepped out of her car a figure appeared from behind the building and she at once recognised the tall, well-dressed man, Ruggiero! They both hesitated for a moment and then rushed forward in each other's arms. Standing there together, no words were spoken but she sobbed gently in relief as all the worries and tension flooding her system seemed to suddenly recede. He was the first one to speak,

"I had to come, Marina, I just could not stand the separation, are you all right?" She nodded, trying to hold back her tears and looked up into his eyes, those wonderful caring eyes that she knew so well.

They turned to walk towards the cottage which was basking in the soft afternoon glow of a winter sun. As they disappeared within, she realised that she would soon be returning to the place that had captured her heart those many months ago, Toscane.

www.ingramcontent.com/pod-product-compliance
Lightning Source LLC
LaVergne TN
LVHW091558060526
838200LV00036B/902